LOLA ST

Sex, Food & Rock n Roll

By Stacey Haber

Lola Steele
Sex, Food & Rock n Roll
By Stacey Haber

A catalogue record for this book is available from The British Library

Published by Hope & Plum Publishing
www.hopeandplum.com

978-1-9160363-8-3

Dedication

To Emma, Mack, Kyle without whom I could not breathe

To David, who reminded me to breathe

To Paula, without whom I can't think

To Marilyn and Cecil, my butterflies

Today, part 1.

I was so exhausted I couldn't tell where the nightmares ended and the real terrors began. Every attempt at movement brought new levels of pain and spasm; I aimed for stillness but each new street sound and every pin prick of light popping from curtained windows as Richmond woke caused me to jump and jerk. I wasn't exposed to the elements but I could still feel the chill of the cold night air; the fright-invoked sweats exacerbated the discomfort. My thoughts were addled from fear but I knew I had to move, to free myself from this fibreglass tomb which became transparent in the dawn. I had to resume my flight to a less conspicuous place. Paranoia that my photo was plastered on the news and in the press was driving me insane. If I were recognised, I would be arrested. Again. By yet another branch of law enforcement.

I normally had a high threshold for pain, mind over matter, but the fear of capture had gripped me so fiercely that I could no longer think coherently; focusing on the pain was almost a welcome relief from the thoughts of danger. I had no tears left but my eyes stung nonetheless, from which hurt I wasn't sure. The two men I loved were already dead and I was next on the list. Capture by either the authorities or my unknown enemy both seemed fatal.

I emerged last night from the Thames drenched in sodden black clothes after the explosion which nearly drowned me and destroyed Josh's houseboat. Am I still a widow if we were divorced?

The cataclysmic blast ended the chase by the Metropolitan Police but it's likely that at least two officers were killed in its wake and a gut wrenching sense of guilt caused dry heaves from the pit of my empty stomach. These deaths would forever be on my conscience; if I hadn't run, there would have been no chase and they would not have been near the mooring.

I had to run. I didn't know about the money or Johnny's murder. I couldn't face another stretch in those cells and the questions from hostile officers who thought everything I said was a lie anyway. I wasn't there to "help them with their inquiries." I was there so they could close the file and throw away the key. Matthew, my lawyer, ended their bad cop/worse cop routine finally by forcing them to charge me or release me. After nine hours of torturous interrogation I was bailed. Matthew extracted me from the cold, sterile environment, painted in penal grey and left to harbour all the stained dereliction brought from derelict souls and the devil himself.

I didn't kill Johnny. I love Johnny. Loved, Johnny, for the past 20 years. First as friend, then as beau and then again as friend. And muse. Every song he wrote was like a love letter wrapped in soft cotton pyjamas.

I could never hurt Johnny, mentally or physically. And he would never use me to launder money. Hell! He would never need that because he wouldn't ever be involved in crime in the first place! This made no sense.

That's how it began. With my arrest for money laundering. Actually it had to begin before, but for me the arrest was the point of no return that set this flight in motion. For them it must have begun with Johnny's hit single "Carry You Home" or its royalty accounting.

I am Lola Steele.

1 week earlier

The grimy shadows cast by the large dirty windows on the vast concrete space delineated the no man's land between the five menacing figures in steel capped boots and truckers' union jackets staring down the suave, suited man. Five men of girth and bulk borne of melted muscles from a more glorious youth stood tense and ready for fight. Or flight. In Dartford, their silhouettes alone would cause fear and panic, a raised eyebrow would signal peril. In the cavernous hangar, with their contrite body language and nervous dispositions, they were merely pathetic, staring at the oil slicks on the concrete floor, afraid to make eye contact. Their body language was a study in petulance.

The sixth man, a tall sophisticated figure stood at ease, surveyed the hard men with a mixture of contempt and amusement. One of the pack of rogues cleared his throat as if requesting permission to speak, his arm twitching in suppression of the instinct to raise his hand like a young student. He raised his head slightly to see if his request was acknowledged. The suited man nodded. "You sure this is enough to get us off the hook?" the leviathan asked timidly.

Matthew Stephens-Gilbert sighed audibly as if disappointed in a child for asking a question already answered, "You still have to testify in court tomorrow. Make no mistake; this does not exonerate or forgive your crimes, it merely destroys the credibility of a corrupt investigating officer. Find a new career, or you'll need to find a new lawyer." The bad men nodded and stared at the floor again like chastised offspring. Matt allowed himself the merest hint of a smirk and turned his back to them, fairly confident that they posed no threat to him as he was the only thing that stood between them and long jail sentences.

As Matt walked through the cavernous warehouse the sun shifted and the shadows followed him, casting ominous shapes behind. He was unaffected by the fear in his wake as he stepped into the sunshine which highlighted the cargo terminals at Gatwick Airport. For Matt it was the prelude to another successful case after carefully placing the last piece of the puzzle when his opposition wasn't looking.

Matt slid into his sleek, silver BMW Z4 and eased the car into gear with barely a rumble from the powerful engine. He actually preferred convertibles but learned long ago that a steel reinforced roof was compulsory in his line of work. He was still waiting for bullet-proof glass to become an optional extra. Although confident his clients were in conclave inside the unit, Matt checked the rear view mirror with more than average repetition as he sped away and joined the M23 motorway towards London. He knew his band of criminals believed him that their testimony would bring down the case against them like a house of cards; Matt was confident that they also were aware that there would be consequences. The aftermath within the syndicate would require new names and a hasty relocation. In their shoes, Matt himself would have killed all the lawyers and hopped a plane as he was already at the airport. Men of their ilk would have new passports already. One of the reasons Matt went to law school was his aptitude for criminal intelligence. At first he shocked himself: young men growing up in middle class Surrey to respectable parents shouldn't be attracted to the darker side of villainy; but he was, and he always silently cheered for the antagonist in literature and film. He found the complexity of their minds and souls interesting. Moriarty was far more compelling than Holmes.

Hyde had much more complexity than Jekyll. Although he rooted for them, Matt loved being able to identify the weakness in their nefarious plans and he relished the moment of their derailment, just to be proven correct in his deductions. Matt delighted in devising a better plan in the given circumstances.

He also went to business school so he could effectively calculate the rates of return and decide whether his career path led him to commit crime or defend it. Ultimately the decision was easy. If he made one mistake as a rogue, he lost his fortune and his freedom; no matter how many mistakes he made as a solicitor, he got paid handsomely. The fact that he rarely made mistakes earned him a king's ransom. He had made the right decision.

The sun rose majestically on Matt's right, casting an optimistic glow over Kent, England's garden, to the east. Its regal touch somehow failed to warm the concrete of Croydon to the north or the highway underfoot. Pessimism was the rule of thumb in a normal case.

White collar crime defence work often earned Matt enemies. Enemies in law enforcement mostly but sometimes amongst the other lower reaches of society. Animals with their backs against the wall often fought back and Matt always pushed hard. He exerted force against his clients because he needed to extract the whole truth; he slammed his opposition with even more force because that was his job, although he did find it pleasurable.

Eyeing his rear view mirror yet again, Matt became aware of a large black SUV with muddy plates closing the gap behind him. Signalling, Matt pulled into the left lane to let the speedster pass. If he did pass, then the driver was just a jerk; if he pulled in behind, then he was trouble. Relief registered in

Matt's taut muscles and rigid grip as he assessed the continued speed of the SUV. It wasn't slowing to tailgate him. Tension re-emerged when his brain decoded the meaning of an indecipherable plate and he braced for impact just as the SUV sideswiped the BMW sending it rolling side over side down the steep verge. Traffic was sparse at this hour of the morning and Matt was grateful that he hadn't taken someone else's vehicle with him into the ether. Had his reflexes been quicker Matt could have stomped on the brake and avoided most of the impact and watched the SUV tumble; he filed the experience away for future reference as he struggled to remain calm and roll with car, viewing alternating vistas of green grass and clear blue skies. He sensed rather than registered competing odours of petrol, grease and foliage. The combination was surreal as was the competing sounds of metal crunching and glass cracking. When the car finally ended its gymnastic descent and the air bag deflated, Matt sent thanks to every heavenly and heathen god that he ended upright. Stumbling from the wreckage onto the dewy hill, he was relieved to find that his limbs worked with a minimum of dissention. Grabbing fists full of long neglected grass and catching foot holds where he could, Matt scrambled back up the verge, the blurred whoosh of sporadic passing vehicles reminding him of a lazy ceiling fan in a film noir. At the summit he surveyed the M23 and marvelled that it could appear so normal after such a malevolent scene. There was no sign of the SUV. Just as surprising, not one vehicle had stopped to either assist or gawk. How blasé had the world become when vehicle wreckage was no longer a spectator sport? Or maybe without smoke and fire there was no money or fame to be had for the phone camera brigade. Today that was in Matt's favour, he thought, as he transcended more easily back down the verge to the car; he thrashed its interior in a frantic search then pulled out a battered and broken recording device. It contained the covert recording of the corrupt official paying off his clients and giving further instructions for their next caper. It was vital to corroborate their testimony. Neither one alone would suffice. After extracting the memory chip which was unharmed, Matt took a £20 note from his wallet and wrapped it around the chip before replacing it back in his wallet and re-pocketing it inside his jacket. If his luck held, the car would be operable and he could resume his journey. It did and he could, albeit after a few false starts and expertly muttered phrases, although it was draughty without windows and the tyres had to stumble over a mile of un-mowed grassland to find entry back onto the highway.

3 days earlier

The Joe Not Joseph tour ended tonight at Wembley. I delegated the gig catering to my crew at Sex, Food & Rock n Roll, the catering company I founded after hanging up my legal briefs. Being a music lawyer was great until I went in-house and worked for a hierarchy of psychos. The company's management style was top down fear and belittlement. A Chairman who yells at a CEO who berates a Vice President who name calls a Director and so on. If everyone was so stupid and useless how could the company consistently score number 1's and be valued at £1.5 billion? And why did no one else see through this bullshit?

I sometimes still work for that psycho company but as a freelancer. I can quit or be insubordinate without fear. Turns out I quit often, so I needed a few revenue streams to alternate while tempers simmered. I now spend my days negotiating the complicated timings of banquet preparation rather than negotiating recording agreements. I spend my nights photographing live music. Although I didn't want to be fiscally responsible for the music industry or the demons that kept it running, I couldn't stay away from the musicians. I would always look after them.

I spent today preparing for the after-party in the old Russian ballroom in North London. It was a cavernous bordello in red and gold, velvet and lame, with a huge dance floor banked by banquettes. I had to build a kitchen in the corridor off the loading dock as this would be the first catered affair the hall had ever hosted. There were however, seven bars that catered to a different hunger.

The menu was easy. Canapés for two hundred for two hours. Mini fish and chips in faux newspaper cones, salmon and tuna sushi rolls with a little extra wasabi paste, mini cheddar burger sliders, kosher pigs in blankets (because nothing beats a beef hot dog for that crisp snap when you bite it), checkerboard brownies (brownies and blondies alternated in a checkerboard pattern with powdered sugar on the blondies for that extra B&W effect), mini ice cream cones (chocolate, vanilla and mint chocolate chip), mini meringues with strawberry or raspberry coulis. Unpretentious food for unpretentious people.

Students from the Brit School were given the generous opportunity to waiter the event allowing them access to their idol for continuous brief seconds. Joe Not Joseph was the number 1 artist who could slip easily from EDM to crooner to hip hop and back again. With the voice of an angel and devilish handsomeness he wreaked havoc on teenage hormones. His lyrical content laid bare their anxiety, depression and unending hope. This trifecta of understanding cemented his position at the top of the charts consistently.

The evening went well; the food was consumed in its entirety lining bellies for the arrival of other comestibles that would satiate other needs. By 2am the kitchen was broken down and loaded out by my trusty crew arriving for a little after-hours party of our own.

The after-after-party found us at Lafayette in the now fashionable Kings Cross section of N1. I prefer dives bars usually but this new haunt was founded by musicians for musicians and had my full seal of approval, especially for private parties.

The interior was currently softly lit with concealed light sources to soften the edges of the stark lines and minimalist décor. The inert, lifeless bodies cut into those lines at sharp angles, the sepia tone casting shadows across the faces rendering them anonymous corpses in repose. Of course, they weren't corpses but the un-dead musicians, roadies and groupies that partied too hard for too long. Click, whirr. I loved the sound of my Nikon D300 Pro camera as I snapped photos of them; it was my right arm in recent years, trying to capture clues to their dreams, the only private places most of them had left after selling their waking hours to the tabloids and fan machine magazines that kept their music profitable or extended their 15 minutes of fame, article by article. My photographs wouldn't aid and abet those goals; they were for my own capitalist ideals: mortgage, taxes, utilities and food. These pics would implement and illustrate a chapter on after-parties in my next book. I hadn't decided if it would be a photo essay about my earlier career as a music lawyer or another cookbook about my current profession as a rock and roll caterer feeding the working masses of the music industry on tour and at home.

As I panned and scanned the venue my lens alit on a nearly empty bottle of Jose Cuervo Gold tequila. As I clicked I never thought about having photos of its owner, Johnny Hathaway, to hawk to his record company in the hope of another album cover shot; I merely shot the scene that I felt necessary to capture for posterity. The bottle gleamed in the glint of dawn stealing its way between cracks, the blue jean legs and Harley boots nearly in silhouette around the highlighted glass. It was a glorious image but would only merit a booklet page or back cover as it lacked the hollow stare and chiselled features of Johnny's million dollar face. He perfected the empty glare from pale blue eyes during the decades of drugs before heroin was chic and rehab was a publicity stunt. If Darwin was right, Johnny was the fittest rocker still on two feet rather than six feet under.

I shot my way up the thin limbs above the boots recalling memories of nights exploring the same route but with less blue material inhibiting the progress of fingers and kisses. I remembered extended minutes teasing the faint hairline from the top of those jeans to the belly button just peeking out of the black t-shirt riding up the still flat stomach. Although my camera captured the easy repose and drape of the shirt, my mind saw a more toned torso reminiscent of Michelangelo's David but softer and downier to the touch. The camera and I remembered the thin lithe neck and the inviting angle it held to tilt the head as if questioning and teasing at the same time. My memory echoed this reality and the strong chin fell to reveal a boyish grin punctuated by the slightest stubble tinged with grey to remind me that this was no boy, but a man that had lived a thousand lives in the last 20 years. As if in confirmation of that pedigree, Johnny's eyes twinkled as I continued photographing him, right on cue with patience borne of familiarity to the process and the person. I had photographed him a million times over those twenty years both for pleasure and for profit. In return he wrote and sang about me, the good times and the bad. Those who say that heartache makes a writer prolific ignore the man that broke the rules. Johnny's biggest hit, Carry You Home, was homage to the cataclysmic sensation of our kisses when our generation defined style and trend.

I remained his muse and friend long after our affair ended only separating myself from him geographically during the years of lost weekends that turned into lost months when days on the road rendered timekeeping meaningless and cocaine rendered relationships fleeting. We were both married and divorced in the missing years, him on more occasions than me. The young ones faded from his side because they ceased to be young enough and the older ones because they hated competing with my ghost. As I snapped shots we sat in companionable silence both single but uninterested in changing that dynamic with each other or anyone else.

As I lowered my camera, job done, I broke the easy silence, "Elvis."

"One. Priscilla," rejoined Johnny, picking up our game of Sex Degrees of Separation as if there hadn't been any interruption.

"Big surprise. Someone young," I teased, "Madonna."

"She's no longer young to me," he laughed, "Zero. Someone old. Tom Walker."

"He's not so old to me," I lied, "Zero. Don't look at me like that. He was great. It ended when I heard a quote second hand that he boasted of the three C's he liked after dinner: cognac, cigar and cunt. In that order. I hate that word."

"Cognac?"

"Cigar. OK, this one has got to be at least four degrees away. Melissa Etheridge."

"Ha! Only one. Stephen Stills."

"You slept with Stephen Stills?"

"Yes. I was young and naïve…and made a pass at Melissa. She laughed so hard I was humiliated. Stephen consoled me until I fell asleep. He stayed by my side until morning."

"Sleeping means sex, not snoring. And I don't think he slept with Melissa either so it doesn't count."

"My lips are sealed. And he left in the morning. Just like I left you one sad, grey morning in Prague"

"I left! You stayed and I flew home." I fake kicked his shin. He faked a flinch and wince.

"How come we can talk now but we couldn't talk then?"

"We weren't meant to be together forever. At least that way. My destiny was as your muse not as your partner."

"You say that, but as my muse you are my partner, in crime at least. I give you half of everything that Carry You Home earns. Spending your half yet?"

"Nope. You wrote it. You recorded it. I didn't help." I begged him not to share the income with me and even refused to give him my bank details for their deposit. Not that it deterred him; he just had his branch at Coutts open a trust account for my benefit and the record and publishing companies deposited money in there. I receive monthly statements which I throw unopened in a drawer. I only spend money that I earn and being loved is not earning, unless you're a prostitute and even then I doubt it's love.

"You inspired it. And you hate it."

"I loved it when it was an album track. I only hate what it became as a single. When they played it to death. Owned by every lonely reject who identified with it and believed it was written for them. They took it from me."

"Rubbish. You big drama queen."

"Rock star."

"Bitch."

We fell apart laughing impervious to the sleeping bodies. Not that anyone stirred. Not that it was even that funny. Guess you had to be there.

"Didn't you get sick of it? Didn't it lose all meaning for you too?" I asked Johnny.

"No. Never. The only one too. They had to take away all my guns after Running Scared stayed at number one. By week 33 I wanted to shoot myself before I went onstage each time. The Snowman was telling me it was the only way to atone for the sin of having made the track. I miss the Snowman."

"How long now?" I queried, giving him an opportunity to boast about his life affirming ride on the wagon of sobriety and clean blood.

"Three years, five months, 27 days and…23 hours, 10 minutes." He looked wistfully at the bottle of Cuervo Gold tequila between his feet. Johnny was saving this last shot for bedtime, whenever it came. It was his last remaining habit after kicking all other vices years ago. One shot a day upon retiring. Psychologically it kept him on the wagon knowing he was balanced precariously on its edge as it bounced along the rough terrain of life.

"So how do you get your kicks now or are you high on a substance free life?"

"If I told you, they'd kill you. Or me."

"They? Spying for her majesty on all your tours?"

I actually represented a huge singer, back in the day, whose German manager did favours for Her Majesty on his numerous appearances on the wrong side of the Berlin Wall.

"Hathaway. John Hathaway," Johnny quipped in a terrible imitation of Sean Connery, "But no women, no vodka, no gadgets. Just a guitar and a smile."

"El Mariachi. 32 calibre guitar case?"

"No. Just Jose. Only gold and only one shot per day. But speaking of illicit activities, how would you screen a potential client for money laundering?"

"I wouldn't. I'm not a lawyer anymore." I was jolted by the sudden change of topic even though the tone remained playful. Maybe Sex Degrees was boring to him after all these years. There were few surprises in our answers anymore whether from ennui or educated guess.

"Technically you are – you're not disbarred or defrocked or whatever they call it. You just don't practice anymore; and lord knows you needed to practice. You were crap."

"I was great. The music industry was crap. Still is."

"Yeah. You were great. Still a genius. When you want to be. So?" his tone was light but apparently the question was serious. I wondered why.

"OK. The answer is: You can't. In my day, taking a photocopy of someone's passport was all you had to do. What does that do? A bit of a farce really."

"And now?" He was really pushing although he was trying to appear nonchalant. More worrying was that Johnny had never been interested in the business end of his career. He never consulted a lawyer to negotiate his recording and publishing agreements thirty odd years ago. It took me the better part of eighteen months to renegotiate their terms when he was a bankable star ten years later.

"Fuck if I know. Why?"

"Fuck if I know. We were always crap at conversation, remember? Can I stay with you a few days while my floors are being polished?" Another sharp turn. Maybe the drugs did damage his brain cells after all and it was now catching up with him. Or maybe it was just the effect of another sunrise after another night of merriment without slumber.

"Do you still have your keys?"

"Of course."

"Then, of course." I smiled, relieved that the moment had passed but wondered about its underlying current never guessing that Johnny's simple question, answered in the affirmative and innocuous on so many other occasions, hence Johnny having his own key, was the catalyst in both our demise.

I had never been a planner. It worried my parents that I was so Zen about life, following opportunities down forks in the road. I wanted to see everything and do everything at least once. The choice to go to law school was a combination appeasement for my Dad, who thought it was a safety net and for me and my passion for all things noir. I had devoured all the Perry Mason novels by Erle Stanley Gardner by the time I was ten, John Mortimer's Rumpole series by 14 along with every private eye novel written before 1975. Gumshoes seemed to scrape a dangerous living while lawyers seemed safe and financially secure. With no other plan in my head, law school seemed an interesting way to put off any real decision about the rest of my life. A notice on the board in the student services office advertised an internship program in London with solicitors and barristers. I applied and was placed with a small art and entertainment firm for the summer and never looked back. I graduated and joined the firm full time.

It was a blow to my parents though. My mother blamed my father for encouraging me to go to law school. She believed that if I hadn't been at the school I wouldn't have seen the notice and would never have been "leaving" her behind in New York. My whole life she said she raised me to be independent and to fly free. Her whole world had always been Brooklyn and the lower east side of Manhattan so she never imagined I would fly so far away. I never imagined I could break her heart by being the person she raised me to be. That was the first dilemma.

The second was the immoral victory of the greater good. I had been negotiating a touring agreement for a singer who had just broken from a super group and gone solo. He had had enough of band politics and the constant battle between band members fuelled by sex rivalries, drug addled minds and competition for the spotlight. As a solo artist he would have greater control of his career and music, theoretically. He was going to be the first western artist to sing on the eastern side of the Berlin Wall. His manager was originally from Germany and had brokered the deal as a peace initiative; the artist had written a song entitled "False Walls." I was negotiating for business class flights, three star hotels and a per diem when the senior partner of my firm walked into my office demanding to know why the agreement wasn't executed yet. I explained that I was still negotiating the boilerplate, but he ordered me to send it to the client for signature. I argued that it was the client who wanted these amendments and it was my fiduciary duty to at least try. The partner sat down stiffly in my client chair. He stood again, strode to the door and closed it firmly. He sat again, at the edge of the chair, leaned on the desk and laced his fingers. He stoically examined the wood grain of the desktop for a full minute before addressing me directly, "This tour…it's important to international relations. There is a bigger picture than petty comforts."

I was taken aback to hear a lawyer dismiss the instructions of a client.

"It's what the client wants. As a minimum, a compromise. More importantly, it's about exercising his freedom and his rights now that he's not encumbered by the will of the band. Whatever his wishes, petty or not, they are paramount to the stand he's taken. Isn't that allegorical of this peace initiative itself?"

His pained face just stared back at me. "There is no peace in the near future. Jonas will accompany him on this tour and will try to rectify it in situ."

"Jonas? His manager? He's never toured before?"

"Jonas was actually born in East Berlin. He still has connections there. He will gather information to help this country negotiate an alliance."

"That's great, but what does this have to do with the contract I'm negotiating?"

He shifted uncomfortably in his chair before looking me directly in the eye willing me to understand, "It will be an uneasy alliance. His efforts will not be openly sanctioned by our government."

I desperately wanted to understand so I held his steely gaze. Then comprehension dawned, "Jonas is a spy?" He nodded and gazed around the room, reflexively scanning for unauthorized ears. I fell back awkwardly in my ergonomically perfect leather chair as if I had been punched in the gut. Was I winded because I couldn't believe I knew an actual spy or because I was devastated that I was being asked to betray a client? Either way I felt shaky. Silently he rose and left my office. I sat alone staring at the contract without touching it or seeing it for an hour or more. Finally, I picked up the phone and dialled the client. I got the answer machine so I left a message, "It's Lola. Please print out the last draft of the Berlin agreement, sign both copies and send them to me. Then book whichever hotel and flight you want for yourself and Jonas. Give me the details and the firm will send you a cheque to reimburse you. We'll recover it from them in a side deal. Let's get this done quickly before anyone changes their mind and makes those choices for you." I slammed the phone down in a rush, suddenly panicked that he would pick up or someone would over hear me. I wasn't sure if I was making the firm pay out of spite or expediency; I would deal with the fallout at this end when the time came. Today was not going to be about letting anyone down or not getting the deal done. Today was about harsh realities and lateral thinking so that I wasn't manipulated or swept into the maelstrom of politics. I had thought I was immune from the ugliness of the globe in my little world of rock and roll. I was wrong.

The third and final blow was the realization that lawyers don't make lives better, they just blunt the pain. I thought that being a music lawyer would mean happy clients; helping people fulfil their dreams and ambitions and helping companies create art and beauty to brighten peoples' lives. Wrong again. Every agreement negotiated is an adversarial relationship ending with both parties having to compromise and being angry - angry at each other, angry at the lawyers. I wanted to be the tooth fairy but I was viewed as the dentist. This was not why I slaved through four years of university and three years of law school. Eventually I left the firm and went in-house to change the system from within, another naive plan.

Being employed in the legal department of Zulu Records was the most soul destroying experience of my life because every right I fought to give an artist ended up hurting them in the long run and further destroying my relationship with my boss.

If I let an artist retain approval rights on their music for TV commercials, their track would never be used in a TV advert. Even if the track was requested specifically, Zulu would say they couldn't get artist approval and recommend another track where the rights were clear. Millions of dollars were lost to the artist that retained control. If I gave an artist a large advance, Zulu would cut their marketing budget; cheap videos, no independent promotion, no tour support. Their albums would never sell and they remained unrecouped, never earning a penny in royalties; eventually they would be dropped from the label, unable to get another deal because they couldn't sell records, career over. When I complained, I was lambasted for being stupid, useless and a pain in the ass. The politics of the music industry was even worse than that of governments.

I wasn't willing to compromise so I left. The company and the legal profession itself. I ran away and went searching to reclaim my soul. First, I found my heart and at heart I was a Jewish New Yorker. That meant chicken soup. It was a starter metaphorically and literally. Cooking enabled me to create and to nourish myself and the people I cared about; writing enabled me to purge the demons that stabbed at my psyche. Cookbooks became gifts and then an income. Photography turned from hobby to work when I bought my first digital camera because it made me self-sufficient, not needing to pay for the photos of food. Other photos followed because of my beloved musicians. It felt like justice when Zulu began to pay for my photos. Soul restored.

Morning had definitely broken by the time I climbed over the threshold into my lovely little house. I was lucky enough to snag a parking spot right outside for my old black Jeep Wrangler thanks to a departing neighbour aiming to be the first man at his desk this morning. I had been driving the Jeep for five years now preferring the square front lights of the old car to the round ones on the newer versions. It was creaky, draughty and a nightmare of discomfort for rattled, shaken not stirred passengers but a dream to drive for me. I had become so associated with the vehicle that within a week I had acquired the nickname of JeepGirl.

I threw my keys onto the small table by the door where a dozen Polaroids of other bands at other gigs sat amongst my photography business cards and my Sex, Food & Rock n Roll Catering menu leaflets. Walking through to the study I deposited my camera on the desk without turning on the lights or caring about downloading the work product before hitting the sheets. On the way out of the study I cast a quick glance at the book case and clocked the spines of the books that shaped my life: Sex, Food & Rock n Roll by Lola Steele, Musical Cherries by Lola Steele, Pigs for Gigs by Lola Steele and various serious gastro-tomes, celebrity chef cookbooks and first edition antique cookbooks on the top shelf; the second shelf contained music related books such as The Hitmen, 25 Years of Rolling Stone, plus vintage back issues of Billboard and Music Week magazines; the lower shelves housed dusty old legal texts, nothing current, nothing opened in the last decade.

I was hoping to add photo essay coffee table books to my resume and possibly bring my income into a higher tax bracket. I was comfortable and happy but assumed, like everyone else that I could be even happier with more earned income, earned being the operative word.

The walls were modestly but reassuringly adorned with my favourite black and white photos: Johnny Hathaway, David Bowie, Robbie Williams, Paul Young, Iggy Pop, Lou Reed, Def Leppard, Billy Joel, Livingston, Fall Out Boy, Joe Not Joseph, Leighton Walker, Gavin De Graw and Post Malone. I had certainly met a lot of diverse and interesting men. There was no one currently on my wish list and I sometimes wondered if it meant I was getting old, bored or lazy. There were also several gold and platinum disc certifications; gifts for iconic album covers. Confirmation that I was an independent woman earning my way through life without compromise or comparison.

3 days earlier

As much as I loved being the person I was, I hated this bit of being me. I hated confrontation. The choice of law as a career was incomprehensible, in hindsight. It was ten years since I'd worked as a lawyer at Zulu Records and I still felt nauseas every time I had to enter the building. I might have been fine if I hadn't been en route to Rupert McDonald's office, Senior VP of Business Affairs and my old boss. Every encounter was a study in conflict. I had tried to negotiate it that Ben Williams, Head of A&R, artist and repertoire, would view my photos today but Rupert wankered it that I had to face him instead. Wankered was a word I made up for Rupert. It meant manipulating events just so that he could be a wanker. His sadist inclinations were boundless and he never forgave me for leaving Zulu after exposing his flaws and ineptitude; his animosity grew when I didn't wither and die, let alone prospered in ways that meant Zulu still passed money my way. Ben allowed this manipulation because he chose his battles carefully; I wasn't important enough to make this a battle worth winning so in the immortal Tao of Sun Tzu, the best way to avoid losing a war was not to go to war in the first place. Ben quoted the ancient Chinese warlord often, an affectation he apparently acquired in his teens. Rupert had a great eye for the right shot and for Ben the end product was all that mattered. It was just my bad luck that Saturday's great photos happened to be of Zulu artists. I never think about this sick feeling when I'm shooting, only of the lighting and composition. I wish I could. If I didn't have the shot, I wouldn't have the burning drive to sell it.

If Rupert was a sadist, did it follow that I must be a masochist?

I met Lettie Silver at her desk after being buzzed through by a receptionist I'd known and partied with a long time ago. Maybe the way to stay in the job was to only deal with the public and not with the employees. Certainly the jobbers working with the execs had a much higher turnover rate. I forgot how much I missed Lettie's cherubic face and easy smile. Even when I worked here I missed it because it was so seldom seen during the work day when Rupert was abusing her over a trivial matter not realizing that wasting her time with a tirade only kept her from the mountain of work in her in-tray.

After a hug and peck on the cheek, Lettie held out her hand. I immediately removed the camera case from my shoulder and placed it in her palm. She deposited in her lower desk drawer near her handbag and locked the drawer with a key. That left me with just my portfolio case as I wasn't carrying a handbag.

"I have no idea why the sight of it sets him off, said Lettie.

"Maybe he's afraid I'll try to take his picture again," I offered.

"He's having a bad hair day with no hair. And he's already in his usual mood. For his lunch I've ordered roast foundlings. He thinks he's being compassionate by putting them out of their misery at an early age," Lettie quipped.

"I should do a recipe for that in my cannibal cookbook. Seriously, why do you put up with him?"

"Same as you," Lettie answered.

"Twenty percent more than anywhere else," we delivered in unison, having repeated it so many times before.

"C'mon. Gimme a peek before you go in," Lettie cajoled. I handed her the portfolio case and she leafed through the black and whites of the musicians shot in various places at various angles the night before. She lingered over one taken on the stairwell of the hotel as a singer staggered three floors below me. It had an odd Hitchcock feel and really captured the depth of the drop to the lobby. The beauty of the symmetry of the handrails were matched by the gorgeous glow from the enormous crystal chandelier lighting us from above. It was one of those miracle shots that couldn't be planned or faked.

"I'm ovulating as we speak," she drooled. "That man's hormones are powerful. Seriously. These are great. Any one of these would make a great cover."

I bowed in a courtly fashion.

"In you go," she ordered. "best not keep his highness waiting any longer."

With a smirk and a nod, I girded myself and headed for Rupert's door. I thought about just entering but decided to knock at the last minute. You never knew how he would react: angry at the lack of respect for barging in or irate at wasting his time and making him shout at the door if you did knock.

"What!?!" Rupert McDonald bellowed.

I turned to Lettie who giggled and then opened the door wearing my best poker face.

The focal point of King's large modern office was a big desk covered haphazardly in files, CDs, DVDs, photos and artwork printouts. An attempt at order was visible but the sheer volume overwhelmed the attempt. It was an affectation as the CDs and DVDS were obsolete in this mp3 and mp4 age. The normal desktop items such as in/out trays, stapler, tape, pens, phones, documents, had been relegated to a credenza against a far wall, although they were expensive and state of the art looking - coordinated and chosen with an eye to style over function. With more pride of place, closer to the desk was a multimedia cabinet which McDonald used to review the elements produced by the chaos on the desk. There were also five large, legal sized filing cabinets with very serious locks. Rupert himself was a tall reedy man who was dwarfed by the breadth of components of his office. He was stylish and hip but in a Paul Smith fashion rather than Top Man high street. What he lacked in brawn he made up for in venom. He was a nasty man whose sufferance of other people mimicked the medieval intolerance of lepers. The guest chairs clearly signalled "unwelcome" with their intricately woven pattern directing derrieres low to the ground while pointing knees up to the ceiling. McDonald's chair, however, was a leather throne as befit his ego.

"Hello Bert," I offered with a facade of neutrality.

"Rupert. Do not call me Bert. As you well know. Lola."

I handed him the portfolio. "Sit," he commanded, taking it from me and indicating the guest chair.

Instead I perched on the corner of his desk, using my hip to slide stuff out of the way.

"Don't start with me Lola," he warned.

Having scored my point, I didn't feel the need to push it so I walked around the desk to look over his shoulder as he flipped through the photos.

"I won't tell you again." I guess I was still inadvertently pushing his buttons but I couldn't help myself. It was my instinct and it was such fun. I reached out, grabbed the portfolio, and headed for the door.

"You won't get paid." McDonald's tone never wavered. I wondered if it sounded threatening when he told his wife he loved her. "Lola," he snapped finally as I laid my hand on the door knob. Suppressing a smile, I turned and retraced my steps, depositing myself in one of the client chairs. Not finished torturing him, I patted the second chair signalling that he should join me as equals. Same seat, same level of comfort, or discomfort as it were. Rupert got up and walked out, leaving the door open. Through the door craning my neck I saw him approach Lettie's desk.

"We're going to the marketing meeting," he sputtered as he headed for the elevators.

I leapt up, collected my camera bag from Lettie's outstretched hand while trading winks and ran after Rupert to the elevator.

We entered the medium sized conference room to find four department heads waiting. Each one was über cool in a different way: Tim from A&R was hip and happening, Zachary from marketing was salesman slick, Mariel from art was thrift shop retro funky and Selena from publicity was monochrome in an indescribable colour that was undoubtedly this year's black. I placed the portfolio case on the table and they pulled the photos out of their sleeves divvying them up between them and then sharing the lots around. I sat apart, not listening more for fear of unduly influencing their choice than from fear of critique. When I worked in-house I saw other photographers push their pet pics only to be rejected at the last minute because the choice always niggled negatively.

Tim held three shots up for the others, "These fit in with the image development we are growing for a new generation of fans."

Mariel nodded sagely as she added, "They're great shots but need a lot of work to be an album cover. I just haven't time to save them. Booklet filler at best." Rupert wasn't ready to let them go and questioned her, "What do you propose graphically?" Mariel immediately took the hump, as she always did believing the visual domain to be her baby and panicking about having to think on her feet, “Oh, I don’t know. I’ll stay up all night and work on them shall I?”

Rupert pulled one from the pile, “Work on this one.”

Tim concurred without hesitation, “Agreed.”

Zachary was also pleased, “Good. That’s the one I want for T-shirts. And this one,” he said picking up another and handing it to Rupert, “for tour merchandising.”

All eyes turned to Selena who pointed to the two in Rupert’s hand, “I’m happy with those two to leak to the tabloids.”

McDonald lay them face up on the table, “OK, they’re not great but as we own them already we--”

“No you don’t,” I interrupted hastily.

“Lola we’ve been through this. You took them while in my employ.” McDonald was using his exasperated voice.

“I’m freelance. And not on your time, on my own time. You know there’s no work for hire in photography anyway. Or in this country for anything for that matter.” I had no hesitation giving a legal lesson to their head lawyer.

“Correct but we don’t need work for hire, it’s a given. Tell your publisher we’re going to audit for the photos in your cookbooks,” Rupert rejoined smugly but stupidly in my opinion.

“Nope.” I started to gather my photos.

“Yes! We could tie you up in court for years. We all know you can’t afford to defend a lawsuit.” Rupert thought he had trumped me on that one as he had so many old-time musicians whose music had been used by rappers in the days before my friends and I, all record company lawyers but one, Deborah Mannis-Gardner, had devised and implemented a system for the clearance of samples which ensured no music or composition was stolen and that a fair price was paid to all recording artists and songwriters whose music was used. Before our system was in place, McDonald and his peers would refuse to negotiate or pay up relying on the fact that the old-time artists were too poor to find redress in the courts. I was still friends with surviving members of The Platters, Parliament Funkadelic and the Isley Brothers.

"Legal aid," I reminded him; although you couldn't get it to bring a case, you could for the defence of a lawsuit.

"You'll never work for us again." His old chestnut which he knew pushed my button as I hated to think of myself as working for him. I did this for me, I reminded myself although it failed to quell my anger.

"Rupert, cut the shit. If you had a case you would have sued already. As for these, technically artist management hires me, not you. So, I'm here as a courtesy."

"I control artist management. You'll be blacklisted." That was McDonald's dream; he was just voicing it aloud, knowing full well he had neither the clout nor the popularity.

I was tired of this game now and wanted to be out of this place. "Then this is goodbye. You keep the cheque and I'll keep the negatives." I took the portfolio leaving the pile of photos and waved to the others.

Not content to let me have the last word even though I'd won the battle McDonald shouted after me, "This is the last time!"

Well he couldn't have it this time, "Just like last time," I said, "Bye kids, better you than me." To their credit, they all blew me kisses, waved and smiled having loved the entertainment provided and the photos even more. While no one was prepared to lose the use of the pictures, none was prepared to stand up to McDonald either. I felt rather than heard them relax as I closed the door behind me. I vowed to myself that I would risk sending jpgs next time even though they could be easily stolen.

I stumbled along the corridors towards freedom. The walls were gloriously adorned with gold and platinum records in simple frames signifying the sale of billions of records and downloads. I passed the large conference room with an army of blue suited accountants built more like hit men than geeks. They were nearly obscured by mountains of files being loaded into cardboard boxes. Next, I passed the small conference room, built for occupation by no more than a tete a tete, which held only a single occupant in a casual polo shirt and jeans with a small stack of files precariously balanced on the too small table. I smiled and doubled back.

Josh Steele was auditing the royalty accounts of Johnny's album sales, as he did every year at this time. Although Johnny was one of the biggest artists still on Zulu, it didn't stop them from playing silly buggers with his accounting. Josh still had the longish hair belying his own days in a signed band but no longer the famished physique of a starving artist or drug fuelled cadaver. His boyish face was frowning.

"Did they short change you again? Stealing pennies and hoping not to get caught?" I asked playfully.

"Hey babe, how's my favourite ex-wife?" he asked as he looked up from his files and smiled.

"Good Josh. You?" I still loved Josh, or rather I loved Josh again now that he was no longer my responsibility fiscally or emotionally. We were very lucky that we were able to reclaim the friendship that predated the marriage. Although I was friends with Johnny too after the romance failed. Maybe it was my good grace that brought these successes. Or my bad girlfriend ways that broke us up in the first place. No, it had to be the former, I was blameless.

"Tired. Confused. Frustrated," said Josh, oblivious to my internal struggle between self-doubt and supreme ego.

"The usual?"

"Quite the opposite," he said sullenly.

"Wanna talk?" I offered.

"Can't. Client confidentiality…but yeah I would."

"Ok. No names, only hypothetically." We both knew whose account he was auditing but it was necessary to play the game. "Shortfall?"

Josh shook his head, "No."

"Then start over because they never overpay," I said suddenly serious.

"My thoughts too," he said "But I can't. They" he pointed to the suits next door, "get the files at 11am."

"Did you take copies?" I asked.

"You know I'm not supposed to without McDonald's permission and he said, 'No.'"

"Great. Give them to me and I'll leave them at yours in case he searches you."

Josh removed a batch of papers from under his shirt and slipped them into my portfolio case.

"Later babe," I said as I zipped the case. I thought I'd better be on my way before anyone saw us together and then found the files were missing.

"Ta love." Josh's stress levels were already audibly less. At least one person was feeling better.

Josh's place was a houseboat on the Thames moored near Hammersmith that he bought with the divorce settlement I paid him nearly 12 years ago. He bought it in a dilapidated state with the entire lump sum settlement and invited me over for what he claimed was a housewarming party. When I got there, it was just Josh sitting alone on the mouldy wooden deck with holes in the teak that gave a clear view to the even worse deck below. Josh, still bitter and spoiled, imagined that I'd take one look at the state of the place and take him back knowing it wasn't fit for habitation and he had no money left to live on. It was manipulative on so many levels that it had the opposite effect. I was so angry I didn't speak to him again for two years, the time it took him to start an accounting career and fix up the boat. He initiated contact with another housewarming party invitation which I immediately threw in the trash. A day later, however, curiosity got the better of me and I put the date in my diary. When the night arrived, I drove my Jeep slowly to the mooring fully expecting to drive on at the first sight of Josh and another pathetic plan that would irritate me. It never occurred to me that I would find a party in full swing, balloons and fairy lights illuminating an aluminium walkway to a shiny refurbished houseboat, the teak now reflecting the lights and stars rather than revealing its innards. It never occurred to me that I'd have to find a parking space or feel awkward and embarrassed at not having a house warming gift. Ten years after that, the increase in its value ensured Josh a retirement income over and above the portfolio he created with his new gift for financial planning and accrued savings; and I was now the creative one who didn't give a fig about security and the future.

I continued on to another staircase and headed to an open area one floor below which housed the accounting department at Zulu Records. Unlike the funky furniture and state of the art lighting on the public floor, the accounting arena was sober and cheaply furnished. The Chief Financial Officer's suite in the corner was flanked by two desks, both manned by perky young things I had never met before, probably named Amber and Bambi or Jordan and Victoria. I smiled at them and they smiled back prettily. Perky number one pushed a button on her desk and waved me through to the office of Edmund J. Van Nosring, the South African money maverick who took the helm a few months before I left. McDonald must have warned him I was in the building. I never did learn what Van Nosring did to earn the title of financial whiz and was now sure I didn't want to know.

"Hi Ed," I sang breezily.

"Hello darling," he responded with what appeared to be genuine affection but which I knew to be a line.

While Ed looked like old money in navy pinstripes, it was the only conventionally English thing about him. Rather than the men's club leather his suit implied, his office was all glass and Perspex including the furniture. There were no accessories, no window dressings – the message: complete transparency, nothing to hide. Ed, however, oozed secrets and lies. He handed me a cheque. It was late, payment for the previous photos they used. We both knew it would have sat there until I came to collect it rather than be sent online. Another sadistic game they devised to keep me humble. It didn't; it only deepened my resolve to be great and indispensable. Still it was money and I smiled and pocketed it.

"I'll double it personally if you get me copies of the ones Rupert didn't see." Ed made no attempt to hide his lechery this time.

"Can't. I've promised them to Chubby Chasers Monthly," I replied joining in the game.

"Triple."

"No deal. You can buy it on the newsstand like all the other perv's."

"Speaking of perv's, your husband's in the small conference room counting your boyfriend's pennies."

"Ex-husband. Ex-boyfriend."

"Still incestuous. Mmmmm."

"I don't do accountants. Never have, never will."

"Ooh. I'm hurt. We can't all be rock stars. Someone has to turn the trash into cash. Josh would never have made it with that band anyway. As least he can support you now – oh I forgot, you have a muse fund. You must be some kind of incredible to merit half. I'm not asking you to show me, just whisper it in my ear."

"I would but it would kill a man your age."

"Would I die happy?"

"No, because we both know you only get off on money."

Five minutes later I emerged from the portals of hell with my portfolio case intact. I always felt like I earned my money the hard way at Zulu.

Johnny sat in the low, sleek, brown suede client chair in his current lawyer's office. The chair and the office mirrored the artifice of style embodied in Jacob Drake himself: dark, oppressive, spare and uncomfortable. Jake, as he liked being called, sat behind his desk which was designed more for style than utility and didn't even try to give the impression that Drake was an overworked, harassed lawyer; rather it said that there were no problems and everything was under control. Although there were expensive artwork and platinum records on the wall, there were no photos or items evidencing that Jake had a personal relationship to anyone. Jake was pointing to pages in a large document as he instructed Johnny to, "Sign here and here and initial here, here and here."

"What is this?" asked Johnny as he took hold of the tome.

"Tax planning," shot Drake's impatient reply.

"Yeah. But what is it?" insisted Johnny.

"We're moving your offshore royalties to a Panama corporate account because there are rumours that the Hong Kong Dollar is going to be de-pegged from the US Dollar," intoned Jake robotically.

"So what if it is? Are you converting my pounds into HKD?"

"No, but it's relevant in terms of the stability of the Hong Kong infrastructure," retorted Jake now miffed at having his judgment questioned.

"Panama has infrastructure?" inquired Johnny purely for the enjoyment of winding Drake tight.

"JOHNNY! We've been through this. Ten years we're together. Five years ago I leave a cushy City firm to open my own practice which is devoted 55% to you. Careful tax planning has tripled your take even though downloads are waning. Now I know that's not because your music is any less brilliant. We know the market is in flux due to streaming and pop idol shite, but the fact remains that you're still keeping more, even though you're technically earning less. So, either you trust me, or you don't." Jake was apoplectic, his body language betraying a stress even greater than the tirade implied.

"I trust you. But now I'm awake during the day, my brain has too much empty space. It needs details to fill it in. A healthy curiosity about my affairs shouldn't give you the hump. I also question everything Jeremy Kyle says…not Oprah though…" Johnny let his voice trail off just to annoy Jake further.

"I can recommend a book that will explain it all so you don't have to pay me £500 an hour for a tutorial. Then you can keep updated with all the tax law changes throughout the world, proposed and enacted, as and when." Jake had regained control of his posture and tone, but not the sweat sitting on his upper lip.

"Fine Jake. Thank you for protecting my bottom…line. Back off and I'll sign. Listen, I'm staying at Lola's for a while. You have her address. Anything else for me, just send it over." Johnny was wary of Jake's state of mind and a little bored with such an easy target. Cracking Drake would not be a noble victory over a worthy opponent today. It made Johnny wonder what problems had arisen with the other 45% of Jake's work load that could unhinge him to such a degree.

"You two an item again?" Jake teased salaciously, incorrectly assuming an upper hand in Johnny's back-down.

"Maybe," Johnny replied nonchalantly more out of obstinacy than evasion, "Or maybe I'm just having my floors waxed."

"Either way something gets rubbed till it shines," Drake pushed, his manner evidencing his comfortable place on the autistic spectrum; Jake could not read other people. Johnny made no attempt to hide his disgust even knowing his expression would be wasted.

Johnny just signed and initialled the agreement. "Don't forget Josh is almost done with the audit. We need to meet with him to go over his report and compare with your files."

"Not forgotten. Next week sometime." Jake preferred to be the one to remind Johnny of things and was miffed yet again, oblivious to his own bad behaviour. Johnny rose to leave and Jake emerged from his massive desk to give him an awkward macho back punch hug. Jake normally despised touching but wanted the kudos of being "bros"; Johnny hated this ritual too, for different reasons, and tolerated it out of pity. As he left, he heard Jake close the door behind him but it wasn't enough of a sound barrier to mask the sounds of the frantic opening and closing of desk drawers and filing cabinets.

It struck Johnny that Jake was not the same man he met fifteen years ago at the Kashmir Klub back when Tony Moore ran it from the basement of an Italian restaurant off Marylebone High Street. Johnny was the secret headliner, the only known artist on the bill and his lawyer had sent his new recruit down to meet the client. Jake tapped his shoulder just as he was scoring outside the Klub. "Hey man, shouldn't that wait til after your set?"

Johnny turned, slowly, as if his state of bliss had already settled within him, and eyed the smaller man in the shiny new "I'm going to a gig" costume of Alexander McQueen black triple zip jeans, Armani black turtle neck and very shiny Italian black shoes with just the right amount of squared toed point and evenly dangled laces. Jake might have been the junior lawyer and Johnny the established rock star, but Jake's outfit obviously cost more than Johnny's well worn jeans and Ramones T-shirt, probably more than Johnny's vintage Les Paul guitar. "Fuck off mate. This doesn't concern you." Johnny pocketed the smack and pushed past Jake. "Um, Kyle Mackenzie sent me!" Jake called after Johnny's back, following him through the door and down the stairs. "So?" was Johnny's only comment. He could care less what his solicitor thought of him, let alone his pretentious little sidekick.

They descended the stairs, Jake hot on Johnny's heels, just as Tony announced his very special guest, "Johnny Hathawaaaay!" The uproar of applause echoed off the stone walls and caved niches creating an exponentially audible din. Johnny sauntered onto the stage area barely acknowledging the audience's ardour. Jake positioned himself just offstage by the sound board continually checking faces in the audience to ensure they were noticing him. He imagined them wondering who he was, oblivious to the fact that they probably didn't care.

Johnny played an adequate set that he couldn't remember the moment it ended. The new songs he was trialling in front of the adoring audience were tolerated but failed to elicit the screams and shouts of his old hits. It left him numb and disinterested in being a rock star. He noticed that the small venue had become unbearably rammed with new bodies while he was on stage and he couldn't navigate an escape. He needed to ascend from this lower plane of personal hell to a higher state metaphorically and physically. His inability to move past the crowd caused a panicked head swivel. Jake noticed and immediately rushed in, for once glad he was small and lithe. Jake grabbed Johnny and pulled him back towards the side of the stage and through a black curtain. The hind side of the curtain revealed storage chambers cut into the cave on either side of a middle corridor. Jake pulled Johnny along the corridor to a natural stone staircase rising to the stars. Johnny's panic abated slightly and he pulled free of Jake's grip, but still followed him out of the underground lair. Topside, Jake ushered Johnny to a little MG parked across two parking spaces on a side street. While Johnny snorted his way to calm, Jake drove with frenzy towards Soho and further means of stimulation and inebriation.

The last thing Johnny heard before the outer door swung shut behind him was Jake's angry voice over his secretary's intercom: "Boxes. I need boxes!"

Johnny left the suite with a wave to Jake's secretary but without looking back.

"Yes Mr. Drake," came the secretary's calm reply. Amanda Durley was an older woman of sophisticated bearing. A widow who returned to work rather than join the cardigan cruise circuit attended by other single women over fifty years of age. She was not yet ready to succumb to sensible shoes and twinsets under Tuscan skies in the company of other widows. Only two to three decades past her prime as first a punk and then a new romantic clubber, easy administrative work in a music lawyer's office seemed the right choice at the time. A year later it felt more like mothering the child from hell than assisting an officer of the court.

She walked into Jake's office with two small cardboard boxes, neither of which seemed a useful size to Jake as he threw them back at her. She side stepped the flying cardboard with ease and eyed the desk, the open filing cabinet and her boss, apparently used to his juvenile tantrums.

"Spring cleaning? Fire hazard? Dust allergy? Ready to finally get storage facilities?" she asked smugly, mentally rewarding herself for not quitting on the spot. Again.

"All of the above. Box these. I've got a meeting" sniped Jake.

"It's not in your diary…?"

"Then I'm just going out."

"Where shall I say if anyone rings?"

"That I'm out. And send those files to storage" ordered Jake pointing abstractly as he ran out.

"Send which ones?" she sang after him. When there was no response she muttered, "Schmuck" to whoever might be listening.

Back at her desk, Mrs. Durley googled "storage facilities fireproof" and marvelled that the word "googled" was even in her vocabulary. She was twenty five years too old for the computer to be a household item. When she entered university, the computers were in a locked room and time on them had to be pre-booked. She studied Fortran and Cobol in her one year of uni before she married William Durley; the idea of university was her parents' modern approach to securing a successful husband for Amanda. She joked she was there for an M-R-S Degree. In the days before top-up fees, it was an inexpensive avenue to vetting a likely earner.

The flat screen monitor attached to the 100tb CPU at her feet barely resembled the behemoth that filled an entire room at school. She smiled at the thought of mastering Word and Excel in a week after taking 6 months to learn how to punch holes in cards and feed them through a mammoth machine.

There were four box-files stacked by the door and one slim package in a first class A4 envelope on her desk. She would bring the boxes to the storage facility on her way home. That was another change for the better since her early days in an office. Large modern office buildings provided facilities such as car service and concierge. The amenities nearly made up for the behaviour of her rude and ruthless boss.

Twenty minutes later Mrs. Durley was supervising a young clerk who was unloading the four boxes from a hand cart into the trunk and rear seat of her car. When he finished she handed him a voucher and got in the driver's seat of her late model jaguar, a gift to Will on his 50th birthday that she could not bear to sell after he died. She knew it was foolish to drive from her home in Acton to the office off Oxford Street behind John Lewis. She allowed herself the luxury because she could still smell Will's cologne in the cracks of the leather upholstery and it comforted her to think he was close, if invisible. On the days she missed him particularly deeply she narrated her journey as if in conversation with him still. Or again. Her monologue was sometimes punctuated by a stronger whiff of musky scent and she knew that Will had heard her and responded in confirmation.

There were several large dark vehicles mulling around waiting to ferry busy executives to meet people in places to talk about things. Even if she had paid them any attention it would not have occurred to her to notice one particular black sedan parked across the road, a Mercedes SLK with very up to date plates, watching her intently.

In the driver's seat was a very tall imposing man, Stuart Walker, a Gordon Ramsay type in build, facial scarring and temperament. The scars bore decades of scowls and grimaces. Just like his mother said, his face really did freeze that way.

As Mrs. Durley pulled away from the curb, Walker eased his vehicle away and followed her at a sedate pace and comfortable distance.

Mrs. Durley drove north then west on the A40 until White City then detoured south to Hammersmith, then Fulham and over the Putney Bridge. She finally joined the A3 towards Portsmouth. She had chosen the cheapest storage place knowing that's what Mr. Drake would have wanted not realizing just how far Hindhead, Surrey was. The collection fee equalled the annual storage fee. It was an outrage for someplace that it didn't look that far away on the map. At least she'd left early enough to avoid the bulk of the rush hour traffic. Striving to make lemonade out of lemons, she instructed the onboard computer to dial her friend that lived halfway between Hindhead and London intending to make an impromptu visit on her way back. They were still nattering away as Mrs. Durley entered the Hindhead Tunnel and lost the connection. Once out of the tunnel she took the turnoff that looped back 180 degrees towards Hindhead and Haslemere. She dialled her friend back as she entered the single lane system approaching the Devil's Punchbowl, a large hollow of arbor and heath to the east of Hindhead surrounded by 1310 acres of parkland. In here side mirror she could just see the two tunnel entrances 40 metres below on the right. She remembered when construction was underway to build the underpass avoiding the Hindhead lights, which every weekend warrior heading to Devon and beyond cursed as that part of the A3 often resembled a parking lot. She and Will had a lovely long weekend in Devon once they finally got past this part of the road but they went elsewhere after that, avoiding the A3 forever more.

She felt a jolt before she heard the crunch of metal as her car careened to the right and nearly through the low metal barrier. The Mercedes edged closer until it was bumper to bumper with her Jag. Engines screamed as the Merc raged forward and the Jag screeched through its brakes. The heavier Merc won the power battle as it sent the Jag over through the barrier and over the edge of the cliff to A3 below. The tunnel holes rose to meet her stunned gaze and screams, and her car descended. The last thing her friend heard before losing the phone connection for a final time was the cacophonous crash as the car hit the dirt sending up sandstorms. The Jag rolled and fell until it hit oncoming traffic and ended its thunderous freefall, obscuring the right tunnel exit.

The last thing passing motorists above saw was the black sedan sailing past the broken barrier neither speeding up nor stopping to help, while the cars behind it slowed to gawk in panic and amazement, various passengers already on their mobiles optimistically dialling 999. Without a road shoulder or stopping place they were half a mile ahead of the explosion that erupted when the leaking petrol hit a spark from the carburettor incinerating both Mrs. Durley and the contents of the vehicle.

When Jake Drake returned to the office later he found it barren and deserted. He hadn't expected to find his secretary at her desk after hours but he did anticipate an hour or two of busy work in the files left in his desk drawer. What he found was nothing. No secretary. No files. Anywhere. The drawers of the filing cabinet stood open and empty. The drawers of his desk bore no papers or files of any kind. Even his computers were gone. He knew that Mrs Durley would not have moved every single file to storage. She had her grey moments, but she wasn't stupid, and she didn't do spite. It suddenly dawned on him what must have happened. Frantic, he dialled the phone. When there was no answer he banged the receiver back onto the cradle and lifted it again, dialling another number. "They're gone," he screamed into the handset, ignoring his pretentious headset completely. His face contorted with rage as he listened to the response that emanated in his ear. "You what?!?!" Jake tried to regain some sense of calm as he listened intently. "You had no right. They are my proprietary information and my intellectual property. Don't think for one minute I don't have backups. Just make sure you move the money," wailed Jake in a menacing tone. Suddenly he laughed, "Threatening me would be a big mistake." His apparent humour did not stop him from slamming down the phone.

Holland Park was tranquil and quiet at this time in the evening. Walker drove the black Mercedes, which fit so well in this neighbourhood, up to the decorative wrought iron gates of an imposing detached house behind a high stone wall. The gates opened automatically as the car neared. He settled the car in the large circular drive near the ornate front entrance. Walker stepped out and opened the rear door for his esteemed passenger, who remained seated in the shadows, only the trouser leg of a fine Italian suit, silk black sock and shiny leather brogue visible. Walker was handed a gilt cardboard box bearing a hefty weight, which he carried to the front door. As he reached out to ring the brass button with the baroque carved surround, it was opened by a uniformed maid of Caribbean descent who stepped aside so Walker could enter. Seconds later he re-emerged carrying an envelope instead of the box.

Walker handed the envelope to his passenger, closed the door and resettled himself in the driver's seat before driving sedately away.

2 days earlier

Nestled amongst the Edwardian edifices housing Chelsea's elite on the leafy side street safely back from the King's Road sat a huge, white Art Deco house with glass block windows and a double wide front entrance. Completely blocking the road sat three blue vans with blacked out windows. As the sun rose in the morning sky, the van doors burst open and six heavily armed police officials jumped forth from each, identifiable only as to their agency by the large letters on the backs of their flak jackets; their heads were covered with combat helmets and their bodies with bullet proof vests camouflaging contours of gender. They stormed with precision to the front door of the Deco house. The lead officer pounded on the door, ignoring the heavy brass knocker in the shape of a phoenix. He waited the standard 12 count and pounded again. This time shouting, "Police! Open up…Sir, you have three seconds to open the door…One…two…three!" When the threat failed to elicit a response, he barked at his subordinates instead, "Break it down." A second officer brandishing a ram rod cut a swash through the others and positioned himself inches from the door, legs spread shoulder width, knees slightly bent. He began his swing of the rod, creating an arc that increased in radius and velocity with each swing a fraction closer to the wood of the door until it finally impacted splintering the heavy wood first and then leaving a fractured hole in its wake where the lock had been. The brandisher stepped back and allowed the others to rush in en-masse as if they were taking Hamburger Hill. Once inside the troop dispersed in varying directions. The last man in was the first to have approached. He stood in the doorway, just over the threshold and dropped a yellow piece of paper to the highly varnished floor. His calm was the antithesis of the frenzied activity of the other officers, some of whom searched and some of whom filmed the search on hand held digital video cameras. The senior officer pulled at the walkie-talkie pinned to his shoulder and commanded, "Report!" As the staccato responses chimed in his hands, he imagined the scenes as if he was seeing them through the cameras' grainy lenses, "Clear!" "Clear!" "All clear!" "Nothing but an industrial floor sander." He adjusted the picture in his mind's eye to a room with tired wooden boards, the large machine in the middle of the airy box of a room, it's coil snaking to the wall, the plug on the floor with its prongs pointed longingly at the socket, ready to be of use and to bring to glory to the old oak underneath. "Damn," he swore to no one in particular, his adrenaline already ebbing. Silently he thought "No rock star to arrest, no headline to grab, no high fives from his kids tonight."

Across town an identical scene unfolded on my doorstep, with the vital exception that I was home and answered the pounding knock. As I stumbled to the door I mentally patted myself on the back for the drawer full of XL tour T shirts that I wore to bed. Right now I wished the Anthrax shirt I wore had a secret vile of the inspirational disease and a secret squirt mechanism to ensure whoever stood on my stoop would bother no one ever again. I put my eye to the peep hole and saw a curious band of clean cut adults in blue flak jackets staring at the door expectantly, as if they could see right through it. It piqued my ire. "Who's there?" I demanded. I watched as a hulk huge of a man pushed the others out of the way and blocked the spy hole with his face. "How rude," I thought. Aloud I reiterated my query for identification but through clenched teeth enunciating clearly, "Who Is There?" The only response was a scowl from the big guy followed by insistent pounding. Seriously annoyed, I yanked open the door as far as the security chain would allow ready to read them the riot act. Before I could begin however, a large man shoved a yellow piece of paper at my head. "Lola Steele, I'm DI Lionel Walker; we have warrants for your arrest and to search these premises."

"What the--" was all I could muster before Walker went on, "We have a warrant for your arrest and to search these premises. We're coming in."

"Badge," I demanded refusing to be bullied out of instinct rather than bravery, as I had no idea what was occurring.

Although smug, Walker was impatient, and insulted that he hadn't intimidated me into submission. "This is England. We don't carry badges."

"Oh for Pete's sake. Warrant card then. You knew what I meant." It was too early in the morning for me to be bantering and playing semantics. He really set my teeth on edge.

Walker was no less irritated but he retrieved his warrant card from a pocket and shoved it through the gap in the door. It forced me to take a step backwards to avoid being punched in the face and I'm sure he felt a little victory over the small, uncooperative American.

I looked at it, stepped back towards the door and started pushing it closed.

Furious, Walker started shouting, "I advised you …" I was merely unlocking the chain to permit them entry, rather than shutting the door on him as Walker had misinterpreted and hoped he felt his little victory slip away. As the door began to open Walker shoved it hard, sending me reeling backwards. I hit my back hard against the wall and the door frame housing the front door to my ground floor flat which was already ajar. Walker stormed into my apartment followed sheepishly by his team. "What? Were you raised in a barn?!" I shouted when the last officer failed to close the outer building door. I cringed at my own neighbourly breach as my neighbours were undoubtedly trying to sleep until the very last minute when the orchestra of their chosen alarms would sound. Shaking my head, I went into my own flat and closed the door silently.

I stood by the mantel watching the countless number of officers begin their search of my premises. Only Walker was still as he stared and glared at me. I heard the imagined whirr and click sound of my favourite SLR as my mind flashed on the frame of his face; I would remember this picture of him, even without the camera. With the portrait immortalized in my mind I needed something else upon which to focus. I held out my hand to Walker.

"What?" he growled.

"The warrants."

Walker handed them over. I wondered if he had failed to serve them would it have been some kind of technicality. Probably not, I decided because I opened the door. Although I wouldn't have if he hadn't said it, so maybe so after all. I'll never know now that they were in my hand. Damn. I perused them first and then took a longer pour over the multitude of jargon and statute citations. I was trained as a lawyer and didn't understand these documents. How did the average Joe cope when faced with this kind of authority? For all I knew it was a fake and a farce. The only thought keeping me from panic was that I had nothing to steal or be conned out of. I looked at the papers again.

"On what grounds are these based? This doesn't say."

"We'll explain that later in the custody suite," Walker mumbled dismissively. The officers who had dispersed throughout the flat and were piling back with shouts of "all clear." "Is there anyone else here Ms Steele?" asked Walker menacingly.

"No."

"Where is Mr Hathaway, Ms Steele?"

"I don't know! Asleep? In bed?" I was losing my patience again. Everything he said made less and less sense.

"Your bed?" Walker insinuated.

"Of course not."

"Then whose bed?"

"How on earth should I know? What is going on here?"

The other officers had surreptitiously backed away and begun rifling drawers and cupboards, opening film cameras, looking at the shots on the digital ones.

Walker clearly did not take the hint that his behaviour was inappropriate, and none of them were surprised that he had stepped over the line again.

"Lola Steele you are under arrest. You do not have to say anything but it may harm your defence if you do not mention, when questioned, something which you later rely on in court. Anything you do say may be given in evidence. May we have your house keys please?"

He's truly insane, I thought to myself, but only said aloud, "Why? You're already inside?"

"We're taking you to the custody suite. These officers will remain behind to search. If you give them the keys they'll secure the premises when they're finished."

Surely that wasn't protocol. "I should be present during any search." I stood my ground.

Undeterred Walker persisted, his eyes trying to burn me into submission, "It would be better if you came with us now."

"Better for you."

"The key's ma'am…now please," Walker snarled rendering the please meaningless.

I didn't move. A female officer whose name badge read Delaney, picked up the keys from the table by the front door and handed them to Walker. I countered her move by striding over to the desk and picking up the phone. I fished through my contacts for the name Matthew Stephens-Gilbert.

"I'm afraid I can't let you do that," Walker said as he tried to grab the phone from my hand.

"I'm calling my lawyer," I replied summoning a snarl of my own and holding onto the phone.

Walker tried to take the phone from my hand again but I held on. "There'll be time for that later."

"I want to call him now."

Walker punched the phone out of my hand, "No ma'am. We'll call for you on the way."

"You'll call for me?!?" I asked incredulously, "I know you don't have a constitution but surely you have civilised laws? Surely I'm entitled to make my own phone call."

"This isn't television. Either we can call for you on the way or you can call yourself from our phone later." Walker turned away allowing no time for a reply to his face and addressed Officer Delaney, "Please take Ms Steele to get dressed."

"I can manage on my own thanks," I said to his back. I was unable to believe his effrontery. Surely this was abuse of power or something.

"Procedure," Walker said without bothering to face me again.

"It's procedure that someone has to watch me get dressed? What is that? Rule 69 of the Pervert Code?"

"You can opt for a male officer if you'd be more comfortable."

In disbelief, I just walked out of the room. Officer Delaney quick stepped behind me.

Inside my bedroom, I threw clothes angrily onto the bed; Delaney in turn picked each item up and searched it thoroughly.

"What are you doing?" I shouted.

"Procedure," replied Delaney calmly.

"Your procedures are demeaning; rest assured I'll be checking your veracity and if I find you are merely just perverts I will be on you until you either lose your career or jump into the Thames."

All the clothes in my drawers and closets were black or charcoal grey – but not gothic. In fact, I'd say feminine. Even the undergarments. I watched Delaney's face as she pawed my bra and panties, waiting for any hint of enjoyment. Whilst none was evident, I instinctively felt that Delaney was not averse to this task and it made me want to wretch. I felt violated and humiliated and did not want to don any item touched by the officer, especially my intimate garments. I stood stock still and stared at Delaney. Delaney didn't meet my gaze but didn't turn away either.

"Turn your back please," I managed without much animosity.

"I'm afraid I can't do that. Procedure."

"I bet these rules were written by men." I shed my pyjamas and stood stark naked in front of Delaney, my bravado a failed attempt to convince myself that I wasn't intimidated. Delaney didn't flinch but shifted her gaze slightly to meet my eyes indicating that Delaney had seen it all before and wasn't interested. I met the stare for a few seconds then turned away to get dressed. Behind my back, Delaney relaxed visibly. I caught the shift in posture in the mirror and smiled to myself. Click. Whirr. I mentally filed the image away.

The large dark vehicle passed the large sign welcoming all and sundry to Gatwick Airport. In the rear of the vehicle, I sat unwelcomely between Walker and Delaney. I felt ill again from the experience and the car ride and despaired at the irony that I was a person without freedom entering the gateway to escape from this island. The location of my curtailment was insult added to my injury.

When the car finally rolled to a stop outside a chrome and glass building of little character I was motioned to disembark the vehicle. The only notification of my location was a small bland grey sign reading "Gatwick Airport Custody Suite." This whole episode was riddled with irony, I thought, certain that this suite offered no hospitality. I entered the building through a steel door flanked by Walker and Delaney. It was a long white corridor, about 32 feet long with four grey steel cell doors on the left and four white windowed doors on the right. I registered that two of the windows betrayed a cheap table with four chairs in each room; each table had a triple deck cassette recorder at the far end. I had no actual memory of walking the length of the corridor only a subconscious acknowledgement that I was closer to the large bench desk at the end, much the way the intervening cels are removed in stop motion animation. I was aware, however that the overhead lighting throughout was harsh and unfriendly, not unlike the faces around me including the newest face of the man at the desk awaiting my arrival. His desk plate read "Custody Officer." The CO looked at me and then at Walker. I became suddenly aware that Delaney had vanished.

I looked at the CO waiting for him to yell or shout at Walker for having brought me here. Instead it was Walker who spoke, "I have arrested Lola Steele on suspicion of Fraud and Cheating the Public Revenue and Money Laundering, Assisting Another to Retain or Control Benefit of Criminal Conduct in the sum of £44 million in contravention of the Criminal Justice Act of 1988 as amended."

My knees buckled but I grabbed hold of the desk to steady myself. I stared straight ahead as if in a trance, finally knowing that the CO was not going to end this farce but rather move it further towards a point of no return. I didn't hear the rest of their dialogue because the screaming in my head drowned out their drone. The screaming voice was my own encouraging me like an army drill sergeant to teleport myself to Hawaii, the farthest place I could imagine from here.

I must have lost consciousness at some point because my next cogent thought was that I had to sit up. I found myself lying on a vertically slatted wooden slab in a small cell with ochre tiled walls and a grey steel door. The lighting inside the cell was less harsh than that of the corridor but no more welcoming in the starkness of the naked bulb. My head throbbed and my throat was parched. I sat up gingerly. It took all my energy to dangle my feet over the edge, and the effort left my head hanging low and my shoulders slumped. I slowly realized that the tiles were not uniformly yellow but faded and stained in places. As I looked higher, I noticed a camera in one corner of the ceiling above the door, and at the other end of the rectangular chamber a one foot cubed window covered in frosted glass with wire mesh. Back at the door end, I noticed a tray sized slot and a windowed slit for the guards to watch anything at any time. I left the music business because I wouldn't cheat, swindle and steal and now I'm the one in jail?

When I regained enough strength, I raised myself and walked to the door. I could hear voices in the distance but couldn't tell from which direction. I banged on the door to attract attention. Either the sound didn't carry or no one cared, because no one came. I felt like an abused child in an NSPCC advert.

I sat at the edge of the slab near the door in anticipation of a hasty exit when the door was opened. After an hour I abandoned that plan. The next hour found me trying to sit Indian style with my legs crossed in the middle of the slab trying to meditate but failing. An interminable time later I realized I was sitting in the corner farthest from the door with my legs up to my chest and my arms wrapped around my knees. My head was buried in my arms and it dawned on me that this was the closest an adult could get to foetal position without lying down. Finally audible was the rattling of archaic iron keys and the clod of heavy shoes accompanied by a gentle tapping. The sounds approached. An obstruction obliterated the slit of the window as keys fumbled in the lock. The door opened to reveal Matthew Stephens-Gilbert being granted entry by the CO. Matt was my lawyer and friend. He clearly came from the office as he still wore his navy pinstriped suit and shiny black brogues, the uniform completed with an old school tie. I couldn't remember which school in the moment because I was so overcome with relief at seeing a friendly face and a connection to the outside world. I stood in the false hope that he was here to take me home but he entered the cell and the door was re-locked behind him. For a second we just looked at each other, not knowing what to say. Finally, Matt sat and motioned me to sit next to him. I retook my seat mimicking his posture rather than retreat to my previous desperate state.

"What's goin' on?" I asked hopeful that Matt could explain.

"Marvin Gaye…Seriously, I was going to ask you that," Matt replied gently.

"I've been accused of money laundering. £40 million. It's insane."

"£44 million. You're also accused of fraud."

"I am? They think I conned someone out of £44 million? Who has £44 million to con?"

"The Crown."

"I stole a crown worth £44million?"

"No. The Crown is the Queen."

"I'm accused of stealing the Crown Jewels? This is really insane!" I was nearing hysteria.

"No. Listen. The Crown is the Queen's revenue bureau, HM Revenue and Customs. You're accused of participating in a fraud to steal or divert VAT that should have gone to Customs."

"Huh? But I'm not VAT registered. I don't earn enough." I was calm again but just as perplexed.

"Actually, you do."

"What are you talking about? I make about £20k a year from photography and about £30 grand a year from food. Books and catering together!"

"Music."

"What music?"

"Do you have any idea how much you earn from Johnny's royalties?" I shook my head no. "About half a million per annum. Now. It was more while the song charted."

"Excuse me?" Now Matt was part of the insanity. I was going to cry.

"You have several million pounds in your Coutts account."

I was despondent. Matt was my last hope for clarity and he was not making any sense either. My precarious grip of the precipice of composure slipped and the tears came in floods.

"Oh Matt, you're not real. You're part of the nightmare. I imagined you coming to save me but now I realize you couldn't possibly be real. I never called you and no one else would know to call you." I was gaining control of my sobbing and pressed on feeling slightly better now that I recognized something, even if it was only my own insanity, "But even though you're just a figment of my imagination, I'm going to continue talking to you because it feels better to have even the memory of you here. I've been so scared and if I can stay in this fantasy then I'll feel safe. It doesn't matter if it's not real. I understand how people lose themselves in a safe place and never come back. I've never had an imaginary friend but now that I do I'm never going to let you go. Thank you for coming." I reached out and took Matt's hand. It felt warm and strong and when I squeezed it he squeezed back. It felt real to me and that was all that mattered.

"You silly, silly sausage," whispered Matt. "I am real. And I am here. I had a word with DI Walker before I came in the cell. He admitted taking your phone from your house and it was opened to my number. After you passed out he decided to call me rather than wait for you to request my presence."

I just looked at Matt. With my other hand, I pinched him. He winced and pinched me back. "You idiot only your own pain is confirmation of your reality." I winced because it really did hurt. Finally, I smiled.

"Walker also showed me the arrest warrant and copies of your bank statements. You really are very rich."

"No shit?"

"Not very eloquent but no shit sweetheart."

"Shit." I was dumbfounded. "So I owe VAT on that? Why not just bill me instead of arresting me? And if I owe £44million I'd need to have over £220million if VAT is still 20%. That's not possible."

"No. You don't owe VAT on that. And this is not about what you did. It's about what you knew. The account has had much, much more in it over the years. Many millions go in every month and many millions go out the next day."

"Every month? But record royalties are only paid semi-annually. Even publishing, well mechanicals, are paid quarterly. So where's this money coming from? And where's it going? Besides, who would give me millions and trust me not to spend them?"

Matt just looked at her. The lighting dimmed. The window slit was obstructed.

"PRIVILEGED ATTORNEY CLIENT MEETING. THIS BETTER NOT BE TAPED OR LISTENED TO," shouted Matt. The obstruction left and the light returned.

"Johnny wouldn't do that. It doesn't make sense. Why would anyone do that?" I knew what Matt was thinking but couldn't believe it, along with all the other unbelievable ideas of the day.

"Personally, I'm guessing it wasn't him. The record company maybe? They had access to and knowledge of the account."

"Could they take money out as well as put money in?"

"If you authorized them to.

"I never authorized the opening of the account. I don't even know how to get money out of it short of going in and asking. I don't even know where it is."

"Only Johnny could have given out the info if you didn't."

"But why? He's an artist. He only cares about the music. If he cared about the money he wouldn't have given me half. Can you call him?"

"No. There was a warrant for his arrest too. They can't find him, though. His house is empty. Literally. Only thing inside was a floor sander."

"Oh. Yes. He was supposed to be staying with me while the floors were being re-done. He never arrived. I figured he met someone and went home with them."

"Always likely. Any idea who?"

"No idea."

"When did you last see him?"

"The Joe Not Joseph after-party. Night before last. We left together about 5am. He put me in my car and was going to get a cab for himself. He refused a lift from me. I expected him and his bags the next day. I even went out for a bottle of Cuervo Gold – he had one or two swigs left in his old bottle. At two swigs he'd need a new bottle…today."

"Wouldn't he have brought his own?"

"It was a gesture."

"It was a nice gesture."

The light from the window clouded briefly again as a tall man in a dark suit walked past. The natural assumption would be another lawyer visiting another arrestee, but that would be incorrect.

Minutes later I learned that the rooms across the hall were interview suites. Seated around the stark table in a faded once sterile room were Walker and the officer who first knocked on Johnny's door that morning. On the other side sat Matt and me. The floor behind the officers was lined with cardboard boxes hastily filled and haphazardly labelled with items some of which I recognized as my own, presumably taken in the raid this morning. One box, however, was neatly filled with hanging files and was meticulously labelled. It was the only box into which Walker reached. I was pale and nervous. Matt was poised, ready for battle. The officers were excited; their faces and conspiratorial glances betrayed a secret joke. Walker unwrapped three fresh blank cassettes, placed them in their respective decks and hit the "Record" buttons on each machine. I worried over the usage of outmoded technology in this day and age. It completely undermined my confidence in the police's ability to conduct an impartial investigation or coherently explain why I was under suspicion.

"This is DI Lionel Walker of the East Sussex Police, Customs Unit. With me is DS Will Bludgeon. Also present are Lola Steele and her solicitor…" began Walker, taking a pause to allow Matt to identify himself. Walker reiterated Matt's name which seemed inane, "Matthew

Stephens Gilbert," then continued, "Ms Steele has been reminded of her rights." I was aware of the minutes passing and Walker continuing to speak in a nasal drone. As hard as I tried to stay in the moment, knowing my life depended on it, my subconscious kept trying to protect me by removing me from the present and whisking me away to a place devoid of fear. I was jolted back to the present by the lightest touch of Matt's hand on my arm.

Walker had to repeat his question, "You're a solicitor is that correct?"

"No," I replied.

"Were you a solicitor?" pressed Walker.

"No," I replied again.

"Then how were you employed by James & Co Solicitors?" asked Walker smugly.

"I was a senior associate," I answered truthfully not meaning to be evasive but merely answering the simple question simply. It angered Walker nonetheless.

"How can you be a senior solicitor for a major city firm if you're not a solicitor?"

"I'm a lawyer. An attorney."

"Are you playing games? Do you think this is funny?"

"You asked the wrong question." I was angry now too. Any faith I had left in the British justice system instantly evaporated.

"Are you or are you not licensed to practice law?"

"Yes."

"Are you or are you not a member of the Law Society?"

"No."

"Then you're not licensed to practice law! Perjury is a crime which I'll be happy to add to your charges."

"I am licensed," I exploded, "You didn't do your homework. You don't know anything about me! Do you? That explains how this ridiculous accusation could be made. You don't have a clue so you're going to shoot first and spin it later. And being so narrow minded, empirical, 'I need chips with everything even on holiday', bloody English. I'm qualified and licensed in New York State. Can I go now as you're clearly wrong about me and you've lost all credibility?"

"Have you ever used an alias?" persisted Walker red-faced, although not willing to concede.

"Good grief. No!"

"Are you known by any other names?"

"As opposed to using an alias? It's the same thing!" Matt laid a hand on my arm again. Knowingly, I calmly added, "No," for the record.

"Who is JeepGirl?" asked Walker regaining his self -satisfied tone.

"It's not an alias; it's a nickname," I chastised, "you don't know anything about the law."

"The relevance of your question?" interrupted Matt smelling a trap.

"This isn't a court. You don't have the right to object to my question," snarled Walker.

"Justify it or move on," demanded Matt.

"We'll take a five minute break," said Bludgeon with an interruption of his own while snapping the recorders off.

Walker stormed out, followed closely by Bludgeon. Matt and I remained seated. I leaned into whisper to Matt but he held a cautionary finger to his lips. He had a legal pad in front of him and he wrote in very small lettering, you've rattled them. I gave him a sceptical look.

They waited fifteen minutes before Walker and Bludgeon reappeared and switched the machines back on.

"Are you familiar with the VAT system?" continued Walker after re-introducing the parties and stating the time of renewal.

"No. I'm not VAT registered," I replied weakly. The down time had allowed what adrenaline I mustered to ebb and I was tired again. The questioning continued on in this banal manner and I lost all track of time. Matt knew I was fading and asked if I needed a break. I declined just wanting to get it over with. I sat up a little straighter and tried to focus. Matt stood up and removed his suit jacket, buying a half minute reprieve. He started to roll up his sleeves but Walker ploughed on heedlessly.

"Are you familiar with the phrase carousel fraud?" asked Walker.

"No."

"It is when a sum of VAT is paid from one company to another, round and round, instead of being paid into Customs," explained Walker.

"I didn't know that. Is that what this is about?" I asked.

"Are you familiar with Xerxes Imports Ltd?" continued Walker, ignoring my question.

I sighed and responded, "No."

"Phuket Trading Ltd.?"

"No."

"Coptic Treasure Ltd.? Po River Antiques? Pequeño Oro SA?"

"No, no, no."

"Then why have they paid you £38million over the last nine months? And why have you paid £36million to Loyal Asp Ltd, Power Gold Ltd and Red Fortune Ltd in the same nine months?" slammed Walker, emphasizing his perceived point score by pounding on the table.

"I haven't! What are you talking about?"

"For the record, I am producing bank statements marked Exhibit Handy 3, from Coutts Bank, Central London Branch, in the name of Lola Steele, account number 5554148. Ms Steele do you recognize these bank statements?"

"No."

"No? Is this or is this not your bank statement?"

"I've never seen it before."

"Ms Steele I am showing you the statement. Is this your name on the top left corner?"

"Yes."

"And is that your address underneath your name?"

"Yes."

"And is that the name and address of Coutts bank?"

"It says Coutts bank and gives an address but I could not verify it as the correct address."

"And do you recognize the account number on the bottom of the page?"

"No."

"No? Do you receive monthly statements from this branch of Coutts bank for this account?"

"I don't know."

"Don't you?"

"No. I receive something from somewhere but I couldn't tell you where because I never open them. I just put them in a drawer."

"In a drawer where?"

"My desk. Bottom right."

"Why is that Ms Steele?"

"There isn't enough room in the filing cabinet." I was surprised that I managed to summon some spunk after all.

"No?" Walker drawled elongating the vowel. "Why don't you open them?"

"Because I don't feel like I've earned the money Johnny gives me."

"So you knew about the account and the money in it?"

"I know there is an account but not where or how much."

"And you want us to believe you didn't set it up, aren't curious about the sums and don't know any details."

"Yes. It's the truth."

"Well we don't. I don't. Do you DS Bludgeon?"

"No. I don't," snarled Bludgeon displeased at having to add his voice to the record again.

"We believe you're a fraudster," said Walker, taking the lead again. "And a stupid one at that if you think we would believe that you didn't know that you are a millionaire."

"I'll conclude this interview if your manners don't improve," interjected Matt angrily. I realized that he disliked being a silent spectator.

"I believe you planned and executed a serious fraud either with the co-operation of Johnny Hathaway or that you duped him for your own gain."

"Ask the bank," I challenged.

"Ask them what? I have what I need from the bank."

"Ask the bank for the account opening forms. They'll show I didn't open the account."

"What difference would it make? A good fraudster would get someone else to do her dirty work."

"So which is it? Evil genius or stupid criminal? You can't have it both ways. You have the statements. You can see I never touched any of that money."

"Saving for a rainy day. We believe you own or have a beneficial interest in several Hong Kong companies – the ones where you sent the money. You controlled it via the internet."

"I'm concluding this interview so you can confirm who opened the account," Matt declared.

Walker exploded from his chair, knocking it over and pounded his fist on the desk as he shoved his face into Matt's, screaming, "I SAY WHEN THIS INTERVIEW IS OVER!"

With my first genuine smile of the day I chirped, "I believe I do. Isn't the phrase "I'm requesting a break to consult with my lawyer?"

Through gritted teeth Walker managed, "We're taking a break" before slamming his hand against the machines turning off the recorders again and storming out. Bludgeon looked at Matt and then at me. He shook his head and left too but in a more dignified manner.

They returned almost an hour later. While we waited Matt requested and was brought tea and biscuits for us. They were brought by Officer Delaney who managed a sly, surreptitious grin although neither Matt nor I knew for whom it was intended.

Walker and Bludgeon eventually returned and took their seats intending to continue the interrogation. Before they could find their footing, however, Matt barked, "It's customary for you to tell me what progress has been made before we begin so I can advise my client accordingly." He wanted to take charge of the interview from this point forward.

"Fuck off," growled Walker in return.

"Splendid," sang Matt, "Lola, this is a no comment interview."

"You smug bastard," charged Walker.

"Just do it," instructed Bludgeon. Obeying the command, Walker started the tape recorders. Matt smiled. I was confused but pleased; I didn't need to understand, for now.

Walker began, "The time is now 19:41. Present are DI Walker and DS Bludgeon, Ms Steele and Mr Stephens Gilbert. We are bailing Ms Steele unconditionally to return in one month. This interview is concl--"

"Matthew Stephens Gilbert here," interrupted Matt, "Before we conclude, Officer Walker please state for the record the conclusions of your further enquiries with Coutts bank regarding the account formation documents and any alleged withdrawals by my client."

"I'm so sorry counsellor, this interview has already been concluded," said Walker feigning sympathy as he shut off the tapes and stormed out for the final time.

"Babe, I'm taking you home," smiled Matt at me, pleased with the effect we had on the bastard Walker.

"Why the fuck did they let her go?" marvelled Drake into his cordless headset as he dismantled another drawer in his previously pristine office. The Office Of Jacob Drake no longer gave off the air of control and aplomb. It now epitomized chaos and desperation.

The smooth but menacing voice on the other end of the phone had a crisp German accent, "Because her solicitor is smarter than you. She was supposed to have only a duty solicitor. You didn't mention her relationship with Mr. Stephens Gilbert."

"We didn't know. At least I didn't," insinuated Drake.

A third voice, Rupert McDonald defended his corner, "Gentlemen. May I suggest we focus on the fix rather than the blame. If they cannot prove her complicity, they must prove someone else's. I think Johnny is logically next in line."

"No way! He's my bread and butter," wailed Drake, his desperation increasing.

"Who needs bread and butter when caviar and champagne are abundant?" Even the simple statement belied the terror implied by the Teutonic voice. While neither McDonald nor Drake could see the man who possessed the tenor, they knew he was wearing a dark suit, sharply tailored on Saville Row. He always did. He was making clear that any scapegoat would do, even them. "And the alternative is bread and water if you don't secure your positions."

Jake sputtered, "If I don't? We are a triumvirate. Wherest I go, thou goest."

It took a nanosecond for McDonald to choose sides and align himself. "The quote is 'Whither thou goest, I will go' and it's inapt here. Your incestuous position with both Johnny and his muse will shift suspicion away from you. My relationship is more adversarial. As your income is seemingly dependent upon his you have no motive. We on the other hand, have insured the lives of our artists – it is standard in all recording agreements. That could be perceived as our motive."

"I'll let you gentlemen work it out. I have a global enterprise to run." The music mogul rang off.

As the battered silver BMW pulled to the curb across the street from my flat, I sat in the luxurious enveloping passenger seat checking my vanity mirror for danger rather than personal reflection. Matt had driven me home from Gatwick and was worried. He had never seen me like this: paranoid and frightened. I was usually strong and insightful, with keen instincts. I've never been like this and I was worried too. Matt shut the engine and it brought me back to the foreground. I was grateful or his over-protectiveness, wanting to walk me in; I didn't want to be left alone. I didn't know how to express my gratitude but wanted to try, "Thanks for--" Matt stopped me with a firm grip on my wrist, his eyes never leaving my front door. I followed his gaze to the imposing Edwardian edifice that once housed a single family before families became small and rare. Nothing was happening. No one entered or exited and my Jeep was still sitting out front in a prime residents' spot. "What is it?" I asked.

"Not sure," answered Matt, preoccupied, "I thought I saw some movement in the window."

The front door opened and two boiler suited men walked out carrying a body bag. I instinctively crouched down in my seat. A Coroner's van pulled up to the house and the body bag was loaded into the van. A uniformed Metropolitan Police Officer and a plain clothed detective emerged from the building as well. I was nearly dumbstruck, "What the -- ?"

"Stay here and stay down," hissed Matt, "Don't make a sound."

Matt bolted from the car before I could object and was across the street in three easy strides. He approached the plain clothes detective and noticed that the other man's suit was more Next than now. Stylish once but over worn and partnered with a box-set shirt and tie. Matt guessed the detective was more interested in finding perps than fashion.

"What's going on here?" inquired Matt casually.

"Do you live here sir?" asked the Detective in reply, immediately suspicious of anyone who had the bollocks to approach a Met police officer so casually, let alone expect an actual response as Matt so clearly did.

"No, my client does," explained Matt, albeit evasively.

"Who would that be sir?"

"Lola Steele." Matt saw no good reason to dodge the question as he really did want answers given the events of the morning. Matt did not believe in coincidences.

"What kind of client is Ms Steele?"

Matt reached into his inside breast pocket and the detective instinctively reached under his jacket. Matt noticed the other officer also had his hand on his hip near the tip of his night stick and was instantly glad that the regular coppers didn't carry guns in England. Yet. Matt slowly and carefully pulled out a business card and handed it over to a very relieved detective.

"I see. Interesting. Do you know where your client is sir?"

"What's going on here?" Matt demanded, serious now.

"I'll ask the questions Mr Gilbert."

"Stephens Gilbert. Or Matthew." The atmosphere had changed. Both men were aware that they were heading for a Mexican stand-off which would be contrary to both their purposes.

"I'm DCI Thomas Cecil, Metropolitan Police."

"Which division?" Matt pushed but Cecil wasn't willing to go further at this point.

"Mr Stephens Gilbert do you also represent Mr Hathaway?"

This was getting eerie but Matt tried not to react. "No. Is he here? Does he need my representation?"

"Are you a probate lawyer?"

"Why?"

"Where is Ms Steele?"

"What does all this mean? What has happened?" Matt received no response from Cecil and recognized the ploy for what it was: Cecil was hoping the silence would lead Matt to speak, uncomfortable in the void and needing to fill the space. With most people it was a very effective ploy, but Matt just turned and began to walk away.

Hastily, Cecil broke and uttered, "We have reason to believe Ms Steele may help us with our enquiries regarding the death of Mr Hathaway."

Matt whipped around and faced Cecil, studying his face for the tell that would indicate a lie and a ruse. He saw nothing. "Death? Johnny is dead? How? When? Was that..?" asked Matt recalling the body bag.

"That will be determined by the coroner," avoided Cecil, "Now I'll ask you one last time – where is Ms Steele?"

Matt turned toward his car to see if Lola was visible. Cecil followed his gaze. They saw no one but Cecil signalled the uniformed officer to investigate.

"Detective I'll need some information regarding your suspicion of my client. I'll start by reading your warrant to search her house and I presume you have a warrant for her arrest." Matt stepped easily into no-nonsense lawyer mode.

"We responded to a 999 call regarding a disturbance at this address. The neighbours heard banging and screaming. When we arrived, Mr Hathaway was deceased. The call is reasonable suspicion to enter and search. Your client is not under arrest." Cecil's tone matched Matt's in professionalism. Ironically, both men were more comfortable in these roles: they could predict the others' behaviour now and knew how to respond accordingly. The officer returned and confirmed what both other men already knew, "Nothing Sir."

"Mr Stephens Gilbert. Matthew. I would be grateful if you could contact your client and arrange for her to voluntarily answer some questions," said Cecil, handing Matt his card.

"What did you find inside the flat? Is that where Johnny died?" Matt was not ready for this interlude to conclude.

Intrigued, Cecil replied, "The flat is surprisingly empty. I'd go so far as to say suspiciously empty. Devoid of anything useful or revealing. Hard to tell with all the mess."

Matt just smiled, "Are you the left hand or the right hand?"

"Pardon?" Cecil asked, confused.

"Apparently the left hand doesn't know what the right hand is doing. East Sussex Customs Unit cleaned out the place this morning. My client was in custody until 5:42pm this evening. She could not have been involved."

"Very interesting," said Cecil and meaning it, "We'll see."

It was Matt's turn to be perplexed, "What is? What's interesting?"

"We're neither. We are the Metropolitan Police. We have no alliance with nor receive any cooperation from East Sussex Customs. They have a separate database and prosecute their own cases – in the public's interest, of course."

Matt immediately understood that there was no love lost between the agencies, something he already suspected but from the other agency's point of view. "Very interesting indeed."

"And your client?" Cecil pushed, hoping that his personal statement would loosen Matt's reserve.

"She has no alliance with nor receives any cooperation from them either." Matt's attempt at humour, rather than exhibit camaraderie provoked a look of distaste from Cecil so Matt added, "I don't know where she is but if or when she contacts me I will advise her to contact you. I would be grateful Detective, if you would likewise contact me with a time and cause of death. You have my card." It did little to placate Cecil.

"And you have mine," replied Cecil dismissively turning his back to Matt, already refocused on another facet of the investigation.

Matt headed back to his car, careful not to turn his head while his eyes scanned the area for Lola. As an officer of the court, he knew she shouldn't have run; but as her friend and lawyer, he was pleased that they wouldn't have to spend the rest of the evening in another small interview room undergoing another hostile investigation. He resolved to find some answers before he let anyone else start asking more questions. Mostly, he was glad to be alone to have time to process the news that Johnny had died and in her building in a loud and violent manner just hours after he was to be arrested by ESCU. No, he definitely did not believe in coincidences.

Cecil turned slowly back around and watched as Matthew returned to his vehicle, noting out of habit the car's make, model and license plate registration. He expected Matt to scan the area, Cecil's instinct telling him that Matthew did know where Lola Steele was and that she might be very close indeed. More interestingly though, Matt didn't even turn his head to see if there was any on-coming traffic as any other person would have done. Cecil also noticed a certain rigidity in Matt's carriage as if he was physically restrained from movement. It indicated to Cecil that maybe Matt was having an internal struggle. He was sure that there was more information to be gleaned from Matthew Stephens-Gilbert, Esq. Nearly two decades on the force gave Cecil the experience to know that now was not the time to push Matthew. Matt would claim any knowledge he had was protected by attorney client privilege, especially if he didn't know what Cecil was after. As Cecil wasn't entirely sure himself, he wanted to wait. Cecil was very curious as to Ms. Steele's morning activities and a little surreptitious digging would grant him the answers to his yet unasked questions.

Cecil joined the Metropolitan police in his teens. He was the son of an army Judge Advocate, who was the son of an MCS staffer. It was assumed that Thomas Cecil would surpass his father and become the JAG himself.

Cecil was intrigued by the military process of a court marshal and its historical background. For many centuries the conduct of English soldiers was judged by the Court of the High Constable and Earl Marshal. It became the "Court of the Marshal" in 1521 however, and the office of Judge Advocate General (JAG) was created in 1666 to supervise "Courts-martial". It covered all British land and air forces at home and overseas.

The Judge Advocate General is appointed by the Queen by means of Letters Patent, on the recommendation of the Lord Chancellor. Although he is always a civilian, he may have served in the armed forces before his appointment therefore the JAG is not a General of the Army; the word "general" instead signifies broad oversight, as in Secretary-General, Attorney-General, etc.

The JAG has a team of full-time judges called Judge Advocates and as many as 12 Deputy (part-time) Judge Advocates. All the judges are civilians, appointed from the ranks of experienced barristers or solicitors in the same way as other District and Circuit Judges.

The Military Court Service (MCS), part of the Ministry of Defence, acts as prosecutors just as the Crown Prosecution Service (CPS) does in civilian cases (except for Customs cases). There are seven staffed Military Court Centres: Colchester in Essex, Bulford in Wiltshire, Portsmouth in Hampshire, Catterick in Yorkshire, Aldergrove in Northern Ireland and Osnabrück and Hohne in Germany.

As a child, little Tom Cecil moved with his family from post to post, first as part of the army and then as civilians where his father presided in all seven of the MCS courts at one time or another. Cecil never settled long enough to assimilate or have a best friend; the differences between Yorkshire and Essex were as great as those between Portsmouth and Germany. As a result, his education suffered and his interpersonal skills developed very slowly. At 18 after achieving surprisingly good grades in his Sixth form it was assumed that he would follow it on with a university law degree and enlistment into Her Majesty's Army. To his parents' surprise and horror, their only child applied to the Metropolitan police for training as a new constable.

Twenty years later, his parents still wonder if he will join the army or go to law school, although they'd settle for his just getting married and providing grandchildren. At 38, Cecil had nothing against marriage and general domesticity but as a policeman he was wary of the heavy burdens the job placed on a relationship. He fled the instability of military life only to find that while police work kept him rooted geographically to London, his hours of employment were anti-social and his professional experiences rendered him distant and mistrusting. Having developed little or no interpersonal skills in early life, his career path prevented any chance of learning them in the present or the future. It was only tragic because Cecil himself was aware of his shortcoming and lamented his inability to connect. Cecil felt no different after a one-night stand than he did after the end of a two-year relationship. No different during either for that matter. He still harboured hope that it was only because he hadn't met the right girl but was cynical enough to believe that in his job, he wasn't likely to either. Still he was what he was, and he had no desire to change professions. He loved the buzz of police work and relished the challenges of homicide, and, most importantly, he was very, very good at closing cases with solid convictions.

I ran. Blindly. In a panic. The Kensington streets so familiar for the past five years suddenly looked menacing; every Londoner seemed a threat.

This morning I was accused of fraud and money laundering. This evening I was going to be accused of murder.

Shit! There was a dead body in my house!! How did it die? Who was it? How could I ever go back there? Was there blood on my stuff? Why my house? How'd they get in?

So many questions precluded coherent thoughts. I wasn't navigating at all and could be doubling back to my street for all I knew. The familiar was unrecognizable. I needed a place to hide and think. I thought best when I was cooking so I needed a kitchen. That one cogent nugget interrupted the storm of silent queries and I suddenly recognized my surroundings. I was just south of Kensington High Street. I twisted through the curving geography and came to Abingdon Road where I knew the chef at The Axis. I popped round the back and entered the service door of the kitchen. Paul's greeting was sweet but hurried. "Grab an apron duck, we can use another pair of hands." I scrubbed and antibac'd, tied on an apron and slotted in the line. The Axis served sublime French food, lobster oil being their signature ingredient; I could see that another hand on the line wouldn't be intrusive and it meant that my attention would be on acute timings and thus clearly focused on non-penal matters. Plus, it would mean Paul was behind me and metaphorically had my back. It felt safer already. While the kitchen door was unlocked, it was invisible to the outside world including all relevant law enforcement agencies.

Service passed flawlessly and the final straggling diners departed just after 11pm. Without any of my cunning or feminine wile Paul invited me to his flat near the restaurant for a night cap to cradle the service induced adrenaline buzz. I was safe until morning. Little did Paul know that his getting lucky was the luckiest thing to happen to me too.

As the setting sun cast fewer shadows over the dingy houseboat blighting the majesty of the western Thames, Josh turned on another table lamp to read the small notations in the multitude of ledger pages in the files Lola brought him the day before. He had been poring over them for 24 hours stopping only to nap briefly, reading them again for the thousandth time as he downed another cup of strong coffee. Six empty red bull cans lay in and around the small plastic wastebasket at his feet. Not trusting himself to lay on his bed, he had a catnap in his chair about 12 hours ago and his neck was suffering for it now. His face showed the strains of a man failing at his task and being punished for it physically. Josh had always loved living in his small confined place with its well defined spaces on the water which smelled so unlike city life, but tonight he was nauseated by the ebb and flow of the current; the normal gentle, maternal rocking of the river exaggerated the caffeine burning in the pit of his stomach and eliciting noxious fumes to his windpipe. The crick in his neck and shooting pains to his head fueled his nausea exponentially.

"One more time," he promised himself closing the files and starting again.

As the sun faded completely the only illumination was a sliver from his lamp highlighting half a column of numbers. He touched the spot with his index left finger and flicked through another folder with his right. The deep set frown he'd worn for the past day smoothed itself upright and nearly began to morph into a grin. Before it could fully form, Josh shook his head as if to clear away the hallucination. He looked at both pages again, let his fingers tap dance over his industrial sized calculator and stifled the beginnings of another smile. “I wonder…This can’t be,” he flip-flopped in his thoughts, “That is so clever. But it would be illegal.” How the hell was he going to explain this to his client? Or confront the record company for that matter? He needed to sleep on it and make sure it was real. If it was still there in the morning and not the imaginings of a nutritionally deprived brain, he would find those answers… somehow.

Yesterday

In direct contrast to the dim shadows on the houseboat, the glaring state of the art lighting in the autopsy room was blinding. The modern digital, laser and mechanized equipment juxtaposed against the old fashioned tiled room where Jack the Ripper probably studied and practised under the watchful eyes of his instructors were no longer noticeable to Charlotte Turner the sophisticated, silver haired pathologist. As head coroner, she assigned herself the autopsy of Johnny Hathaway, worried that the younger generation would not pay venerable homage to the 'aged' rock legend. Hathaway was ten years younger than Turner herself but the rock and roll lifestyle had added years; to a generation half her age, Hathaway and Turner looked the same era, especially now that Johnny didn't have the benefit of hip and trendy clothing to skew the image.

Turner's respectful inspection of Hathaway's inner workings was nearly complete, the charred and shrivelled organs removed and sliced for technical analysis in labs that would confirm what she already suspected.

To the invisible voice-activated recording system she continued, "Stomach contents indeterminate due to caustic erosion. Five grams of liver for content analysis in bag number 3A87/05 sealed at 08:13."

When the bagging and tagging of internal organs was complete, Turner stood very still eyeing the once famous corpse. A look of perplexity revealed that there were still questions not yet answered. She moved toward Johnny's head. Her gloved fingers traced the dry spots and scabs on his lips. Rather than being romantic as it appeared at first glance, it was clinical. She sliced and bagged one of the scabs, then pried open his jaw and reached for the penlight torch that hung suspended overhead. She shined it into the oral and nasal cavities following the beam with her steely penetrative gaze. Eventually she reached for some instruments and scraped cells from the nose and teeth placing them in separate bags. "Oral and nasal passages reveal the same corrosive onset as the internal organs. Dentition scrapings reveal the least erosion and appear to be some as yet unidentified protein. Bags are marked and identified as 3A88/05 and 3A89/05 respectively. 08:56." Turner repeated the procedure penetrating the light and a laser deep into his throat, then retreating to his fingernails and hair. A gentle sweep of the long unruly locks revealed thin raw patches of scalp. "Four patches on the rear cranium are consistent with fingers grasping the hair to pull the head backwards. Possible indication of force to ensure ingestion of caustic liquid." Turner respectfully replaced the greyed waves of hair. Whatever injustices she had yet to perform upon the corpse, she wanted the face to remain as it should in her memory.

Four hours later, Dr Turner was back in her office. It was pleasant but minimalist. While Charlotte could retain the names of every muscle, bone, neural passage and the million other intricacies of the human body and the items that caused its cessation, she found she couldn't focus in a cluttered environment. It took seven years and seventy negotiations for her to earn the clout to take the neighbouring office under secondment as a file room. In her first five years at the London Coroner's office, she made her secretary keep every scrap of paper and office supply in the outer area to the point where files and supplies were blocking every means of ingress and egress.

Turner's desk only ever held three items, her laptop, phone and the file she was speaking about. When she wasn't on the phone, it went into a drawer leaving only two items. Occasionally a yellow post it note would emerge from the dozens in her pockets to remind her of an afterthought that didn't form part of the autopsy record and only occurred to her after the surgery.

The three necessary items in place, Turner dialled DCI Cecil's mobile phone.

The shrill sound of an old ring tone pierced the ambient burble of voices on the busy London shopping street. Cecil quickly reached into his pocket to retrieve the phone and end the noise as he ducked and dived around pedestrians and into doorways. He wore a moth eaten tweed flat cap and nondescript sunglasses which were as anonymous as his grey slacks and button down shirt. Glancing at the screen of his phone, Cecil answered in the middle of the third ring. "Did you nail it? Time? Cause?"

Turner was used to the peremptory questions preceding the niceties of conversation and was equally as happy to get straight to the point. "Cause is bleach. Ordinary household bleach. Ingested, in or with, tequila."

"Not your usual rock and roll cocktail," mused Cecil as he turned a corner and pulled immediately back. Glancing surreptitiously around the corner, Cecil watched the woman he was tailing approach a well-known accessory shop.

"Not likely. It would explain smashed guitars and hotel rooms though. I found worm remains on his teeth and no food in his stomach. What was left of the stomach anyway. Also some bald spots on the back of his head indicating he was force fed spiked tequila. By the time it got to the bottom of the bottle he would be convulsing, hence biting the worm."

"So not a delicacy."

"No a very violent painful death.

"The fight heard by the neighbours?"

"Initially a fight with his attackers; then his own thrashing. The pain from the bleach burning his insides would have been excruciating."

"Time of death?" asked Matt as he rounded the corner, his quarry safely ensconced in the store.

"Approximately 3-5pm. Probably as the neighbours were calling it in. There's more. The dentition sample also revealed haemoglobin and epidermis – blood and skin."

"The worm was alive? How?"

"No it was pickled. This is human. But no DNA match on our system."

"Meaning no priors, no paternity suits, no immigration files, no childbirth."

"It was male."

"Narrowing down the field to only 7 mil – Gotta go." Cecil hung up the phone abruptly, his perp was on the move again. He followed her through the throng of shoppers.

The warmth of Paul's body was reassuring as a sentience of danger intruded my slumber. I slept fitfully until I found the cradle of his arm. The chase dreams felt all too real.

I had turned off my phone because all the movies tell you that it can be GPS tracked but I needed to know what was happening before I could decide how to proceed. Although I was safe here now, it wouldn't last if my face was splattered all over the news as a murderous lunatic master criminal. Finding Paul's house phone I called Matt's office and learned he was seeing a client; he was not expected back at the office today. I didn't want to call his mobile in case it was bugged. For that matter I'd better get off the land line too just to err on the side of caution.

I borrowed a new black T-shirt from Paul undertaking the best mimicry of my cleansing ritual as possible in a lad's bathroom and set off for Waterloo Station. I picked up Paul's hat and sunglasses just to gild the lily. I was still ignorant about the extent of my fugitive status but I kept my head down and my pace brisk. At Waterloo I boarded a Portsmouth train heading southwest. Disembarking at Guildford my heart rate quickened when I saw a manned barrier impeding my exit. In my fear I had missed the fully automated gates but now quickly detoured to them. I blended in with a crowd of students dressed similarly in dark jeans and T's and let myself be herded along with them to the city centre. I stopped in front of Starbucks now wearing the hat and sunglasses. I was near frantic from my night on the lam and being out in public again. I felt as if every pair of eyes bore into my back lasering "Guilty" in scarlet letters.

Cecil's chase led him to Starbucks and he nearly crashed into her. He mumbled, "Scuse," and pulled his cap lower. Cecil walked on, nearly to Kensington High Street tube Station before doubling back and resuming his watch. He was lucky that the black widow ventured into the coffee bar and took a window seat to enjoy her cappuccino.

I peered through the window of Starbucks on Market Street in Guildford. I had never been to Guildford before and was confused by the same branded shops in differing configuration from my own neighbourhood. I asked one of the students for directions to Starbucks as I disembarked from the railway train. He led me to a small coffee bar on the corner of Lion's Walk and the High Street. There was no sign of Matt and after loitering for ten minutes, the barista directed me to the larger version halfway up the hill closer to North Street. If he wasn't there, I would have to trudge all the way up the hill to the third and even bigger one. It amazed me that a town I'd never heard of or been to would be large enough to merit three Starbucks as well as two Cafe Nero's and at least one Costa coffee, that I could see. I guessed that it was an affluent part of Surrey not only because of the quantities of high price coffees consumed but because of the plethora of designer shops in between each coca bean fuelling station.

At the second Starbucks, I peered in through the window. To the patrons inside, it looked as if the woman staring in through the window was debating with herself whether to enter and have an overpriced but extremely delicious coffee, until I started banging on the window. I spotted Matt sitting in a lush leather armchair in front of a small round pine table. Across from him sat an over dressed, over accessorized, overly blond woman of advanced, but well preserved age in a matching comfy chair. Matt looked up at the same time as most of the other patrons. I saw him speak to the woman and stride towards the door.

Before the door even closed behind him, he started to speak in a rush, "Where have you been? Why are you here? I am obligated to call the police you know."

"I'll be gone before you finish dialling," I warned. "Sorry to interrupt your date."

Already exasperated Matt corrected, "Meeting. Not date. Client not girlfriend."

Sheepishly I said, "Oh," not even sure why I jumped to that conclusion. It was the middle of a work day and it was none of my business. Why did I care and why was I embarrassed?

Again Matt asked, "Why are you here?"

"I want, need, to know what's happening?"

"I'm sorry," Matt paused. I assumed he either didn't have any news or felt bad for going about his business even though my world had stopped. Matt took a breath and rushed out, "Johnny's dead. He died in your flat and the police want to question you." Matt's annoyance ebbed as he delivered the terrible news.

"What? No. Dead? How? NO!" The rush of emotions rocked me and my shouting gave way to sobbing. The shock of my arrest, the exhaustion of being on the run and the grief from this news were too much for me. Matt pulled me close without hesitation, backed me away from the gawking eyes of Starbucks and held me as the sobbing turned to shaking. "This can't be happening. It can't. It's insane."

"I'm sorry. I know you cared about him. I don't have any other information yet. Let me take you to New Scotland Yard. We'll ask all your questions."

Suddenly there was a loud cracking sound, the world exploded and the air around our heads vibrated. My hat was blown from my head. The window behind us crashed cascading us with glass shards. Instinctively we ducked. Matt yanked my arm and we ran still crouched away from the High Street towards North Street. Another shot whizzed past us and a window across North Street shattered. Shoppers began running and screaming.

We ducked into the large multi-levelled sports shop on the corner. There was a huge fabricated mountain in the middle of the shop scaling two stories with a waterfall cascading down the front. Running to the other side gave us a moment's cover before the mountain itself came crashing down and the shop was flooded, the wave dragging us out the front door, along with several other innocent shoppers.

"Surely I don't warrant a shoot to kill order! This is insane!" I wouldn't have believed the police would fire without warning at a fugitive in a civilian crowd. It made no sense.

"He's not authorized and he's probably after me." Matt pulled a fob from his pocket and pushed a button. His Silver BMW sprang to life. He shouted, "Get in!" to me nearly shoving me to the passenger side of the car. Before I could pull my door closed or buckle up, Matt had the car in reverse nearly swiping the dark Mercedes next to him with the BMW's nose. Possessed, Matt manoeuvred his car in total disregard of the other vehicles leaving a trail of tires screeching and cars crashing behind us. Bullets followed us the length of North Street until Matt turned out of the centre of Guildford toward the highway. He careened the sleek vehicle around the crowded streets of Guildford. I tried to speak but Matt silenced me with a flick of his hand.

I fumed but kept my silence as he had just saved my life. I think.

Matt pulled his mobile phone from an inside pocket and dialled with one hand, causing erratic, high speed driving with the other as he headed for the A3 towards London. I finally managed to secure my seat belt after being thrown side to side as if in a bumper car at a fun fair rather than running from a homicidal maniac with a gun. I freaked, emitting a high pitched shriek, thinking about Johnny being dead and me being next, until Matt hissed at me.

"Shh. I'm on the phone," His manner changed sudden and abruptly, "Mrs. Hawks. Matthew…Yes it was very scary. Something has come up. Can we reschedule please? Would you be able to attend my office tomorrow? Thank you. And would you bring my briefcase with you please? You're very kind. Thank you."

Matt clicked off one call and started another. As he dialled the last 9 of 999 the BMW was rear ended by an SUV. He nearly dropped the phone but managed to secure his grip on it; having done so he hurled it into my lap. The politeness of his phone manner had used up his reserve of civility. I looked at the screen, the call hadn't gone through. I started to dail but kept hitting the wrong buttons as the car swerved. Matt kept speeding up and changing lanes. So did the SUV turning this into a high speed car chase. The SUV followed us onto the A3. For seven miles Matt swerved and scraped managing to avoid giving the SUV a clear shot with either bullets or bumpers. At the last minute, Matt veered left and headed for the

M25 north. The SUV missed the exit, but the blaring of horns and screeching of tires signalled that it was reversing to the exit and would be in hot pursuit again soon.

The chase ensued on the M25 within minutes, and soon the SUV was alongside the BMW. The passenger window of the SUV opened and the shooter aimed for Matt at close range. The bullet shattered the rear driver's side window as Matt put pedal to the metal and surged the BMW forward. The shooter tried aiming at the car's tires instead but Matt changed tactics again this time changing lanes and putting more vehicles between them. The SUV finally managed to pull close again and the driver tried sideswiping the BMW but Matt jammed on the brakes and the SUV went ahead of us in our lane. I saw Matt manoeuvre to rear end them and try to disable them, thus ending the chase once and for all but he changed his mind at the last minute, not sure his vehicle would emerge the victor of that encounter. The other cars on the road were becoming savvy to the danger and pulled away to give us space and keep a safe distance. I could just make out handsets to ears and hoped that they were calling 999 to report the incident. At least three vehicles got caught in between us and the SUV and were made to crash, roll and burn. I was terrified for myself and Matt as well as for all the other people on the road at that minute. I looked over at Matt and gauged his total concentration. He must have noticed my movement peripherally because he demanded, "Lola, what the hell is going on?"

How dare he? Angrily I answered, "I don't know. I asked you that yesterday."

"Why did you run? What do you know and what are you hiding from me?"

"I don't know. Nothing! I just panicked. There were cops at my door again and I didn't want to be arrested. Again. It's terrifying."

"This is more terrifying."

"I'm sorry but I'll probably freak every time someone knocks on my door now. I'm probably going to freak now without the knocking."

"Get therapy."

"Get stuffed." I'd never seen Matt like this. He felt like an enemy. I wasn't sure how anyone else would react in this situation but I was no longer sure whether he was one of the good guys or bad guys.

"We're going to Scotland Yard. This is serious. Dial 999. Who the hell are they? They're professional."

"Professional what? How did they know where I was? Maybe it's their money I supposedly stole. No. It's the Queen's money. The Queen is trying to kill me?!?"

"Lola stop that. Focus. What were you doing in Guildford?"

"Looking for you. Your secretary said you were meeting someone."

"Hmm."

"What does that mean?"

"Where were you last night?"

"If I tell you I can't go back there."

"Ok. Were you followed? Who knows about that place?"

"I have no idea. But if anyone knew, they could have shot me in my sleep."

"True. Why didn't you just call me?"

"I was afraid my phone was bugged."

"That's it. That's my girl," Matt said smiling and sounding more like himself. Matt shouted, "Ring Office." His car phone was voice activated. Cool. If he had a car phone, why had he used a mobile phone?

"Hi Lauren. I'm not satisfied with our current cleaners. Please arrange for the old company to re-quote today. They can come after the current company finishes tonight. Get me a grime report ASAP. Thanks…Not sure. I'll be out of touch for a while. Mrs. Hawks will be in tomorrow. Can you fit her in late and let us both know the time. She'll have my briefcase. Ok. I'll call you." Matt turned towards me, indicated his mobile and continued, "Turn the phone off and remove the SIM chip." I did. Matt removed his ear piece and handed it to me. "Throw them out of the window."

"Now?" I asked.

"Right now," ordered Matt.

I lowered my window with the electronic button and flung them just as the SUV pulled up alongside, its driver side window down in readiness for another shot. The ear piece flew into his face causing him to remove his hands from the wheel; his flailing arms knocked into the sniper rifle held by the passenger letting a bullet lose in the SUV ricocheting against the interior. Matt sped away towards the M4 Heathrow exit and we heard the crash behind us.

Matt exited the M4 at Chiswick not wanting to become embroiled in the traffic that was bound to build up on the next flyover. As we neared the roundabout an idea struck him. He drove the BMW calmly and casually into the Porsche dealership at the base of Gunnersbury Road.

I looked at him questioningly and he simply said, "Follow my lead." Obligingly I exited the vehicle after him and started looking at the Porsches on display in the forecourt.

In his friendliest voice of the day Matt asked me, "What colour do you like honey?"

I couldn't shake off the fright and heartache of the preceding minutes as easily but I tried to smile as I said, "Black darling."

With a chuckle Matt mumbled, "Why did I even ask?" I looked at him to see if he was being vicious or attempting humour. I recognized the twinkle and unclenched the fist I didn't realize I was holding.

"Maybe I need to rethink my wardrobe," I said in a whisper, but aloud I replied, "Red schnookums."

In a whisper Matt said, "Yes. That's much more conspicuous."

"More?" I queried in a stage whisper.

"Hide in plain sight I'm thinking."

A shiny suited salesman approached eyeing us both head to toe. I returned the favourable glance although I was thinking that if he did own a Porsche of his own, all his money went on the car rather than on a stylist.

"Good afternoon Sir," he said to Matt, saving only a wink for me, "How can I help you today? Or is it for the Mrs?"

"It's for me. I'm ready to trade up. And it's Matthew. Not Sir."

"Splendid," the salesman said rubbing his hands unconsciously.

Matt gave him a raised eyebrow that said, "Don't play me for a sucker." The salesman dropped his hands and turned bright red.

"Right. That's great Matthew. Which model were you thinking?"

"Not sure. Which is the most popular?"

"The Boxster. Not the highest performance but the best babe mag – Sorry miss," as his face did a beetroot impression.

I had the vague notion it might be his first day and instantly felt sorry for him, "Maybe I'll borrow it then."

Rather than amuse him, I embarrassed him further and he began to cough and sputter, "Uh. Um. It's also the best value for money if you're keeping it in London; less to fear from other drivers and thieves," he said trying to regain his composure.

"Which colour is the most popular?" asked Matt.

"Crimson – sorry red."

"Just what I wanted to hear. Show me, I mean us," corrected Matt.

The salesman walked them over to a row of identical red Boxters.

Matt turned to me, "Beautiful aren't they honey?" To the salesman he said, "How about a lifestyle compatibility test?"

"A man who knows. No problem. I'll sort it right out. Your car keys please." Matt handed over his car keys. I looked on bemused as the salesman walked back inside to his office.

"Lifestyle compatibility?"

"Two day test drive."

"What pretentious crap." Matt just smiled as the salesman came back with the Porsche keys and his business card which he handed to Matt.

"Enjoy the ride. Call me if there are any problems. But there won't be," he said with a wink, "Sorry Matt, habit." Matt just shook his head as he shook his hand.

I waved as we entered the shiny new car and drove off the lot.

"He didn't even ask you for ID. Or to sign anything." It sounded like a statement but it was obviously a question.

"He has my car. My registration. My fingerprints. All the info and ID he needs. He'll be online right now getting all my details." Matt was feigning nonchalance but he was amused to know something I didn't.

"What if the Beemer was stolen and you're not you?"

"I'd be wearing gloves. And I'd probably be alone, or you'd be showing cleavage."

"That's it?"

"That's it. A calculated risk to sell an expensive thing that nobody needs. The percentages are on their side. Less risky than trusting you with £44million."

"Funny. So now what?" I was not happy that the conversation had turned back to my awful predicament. I wished I really was the silly wife of a man who would drive a midlife crisis car and not the accused muse of a newly deceased singer who may or may not have betrayed my love and trust.

"We drive to Porsche-ville and blend in, giving us time to gather information and assess."

To me that sounded much better than driving to Scotland Yard to turn myself in. I had no idea why Matt had this sudden change of heart but I wasn't going to push the point or spoil the mood.

Rupert McDonald was seated at his throne eyeing and pawing the items on his desk, ignoring his guest. The uncomfortable occupant of the torture chair was Josh Steele, a legal pad on his lap and biro in his hand. Josh refused to acknowledge King's cold shoulder and the hint that his presence was unwelcome. Josh exhibited no signs of discomfort caused by either the host or the horrible furniture and pressed on with his questions, "Who authorized the use of the royalties for stock purchases in Albania? In fact, where are the sales invoices for the Albanian retailers? I also need the recoupment breakdown."

"You have a copy of the recording agreement and the outline," intoned McDonald. "There are no holdbacks on recoupment and we don't need artist approval in currency controlled territories."

"Recoupment still has to be itemized," argued Josh, "Someone here had to authorize the purchases – although we don't agree about the approval waiver. Either way I want to speak to whoever authorized the purchases to understand the deal and determine whether royalties were lost or earned in the resale. I want the invoices because Albania isn't a signatory to any copyright convention and I want to know who is accounting for royalties. I understand why they would – top dollar for genuine product, not cheap bootlegs – but I want to keep track of any changes in the future."

Although McDonald wasn't inclined to speak in response, he never had the opportunity as Jake Drake stormed in, nearly busting the office door with his fury. Lettie followed closely and angrily pulled at his collar. She would have yanked him by his hair but she wasn't tall enough to reach.

"Hold it right there. I said he's in a meeting," she snarled.

Wrenching himself from her grip he growled, "And I said it couldn't wait."

McDonald jumped to his feet, although it was unclear to whose aid he was leaping. "What the fu – Josh, I'll have Lettie get you the Albania files. Will you excuse us please?" Josh looked from one to the other to the third. McDonald and Drake were locked onto each other with deadly stares. Lettie was furious at both of them, Drake for disrespecting her authority and McDonald for not enforcing his own commands. Josh was simmering an anger of his own.

"I don't believe this. Now Rupert. I want them now."

"Right now. Lettie please give Josh anything he needs." McDonald had his temper under control again and was exuding a conciliatory tone for someone's benefit.

Lettie would rather have kept hold of Drake and thrown him off the roof. She was used to McDonald changing his orders with each breath and she decided not to choose this battle. Silently she turned on her heel and left. Josh reluctantly exited with her.

McDonald came out from behind his desk and closed the door behind them. He then turned towards Drake in a manner which seemed placatory but when he was within arm's length he slapped Drake across the faces leaving a red handprint. The slap was effeminate but the force was strong. The duality confused and humiliated Drake.

"Get hold of yourself," hissed McDonald. "Under no circumstances may you do that again."

"Where do you get off?" Drake shrilled in reply, "I don't work for you, I work with you. I certainly don't take orders from you. If you'd have hit me like a man, I'd have thrown you out of that window already. I was put off by that pussy slap."

"Charming. Now what are you doing here causing a memorable scene?"

"My files and my secretary are missing. My star client is dead. More importantly my bank account is missing your last payment." The angrier Drake got, the calmer McDonald felt.

"I suggest you find what you've lost or else you've lost your only leverage. As for payments, there'll be no more until the inquest on Johnny is concluded. Then we'll do a final audit and re-jig to post termination accounting."

"Don't give me that shit Rupert. Post termination the royalties decrease. If he or his estate gets less, you and I get less."

"Then we get less. I'm bound by the contract."

"Bullshit. I negotiated that agreement. The sunset clauses are for early termination or expiration. Death isn't included because you're covered by the life insurance. You're up to something."

"You're up to something. Your eyeballs. Your problems are your own. If you're short of cash, see your bank manager."

"This isn't over. I have two other artists on your roster. You up the marketing spend and tour support and they could be earning enough to justify that income in six months. Business as usual."

"Not interested. I'm bored. I have enough"

"It's not up to you. Or me. We're a cartel. A conspiracy if you like. Shall I call from here for a third opinion?" Drake reached out for McDonald's phone assured that McDonald would not want Drake to place the call. When McDonald didn't so much as twitch, Drake assumed he was calling what he thought was a bluff. He paused long enough for McDonald to smirk then heatedly punched in the digits. After a second he heard the familiar voice, "This can't wait. We've been cut off. Rupert thinks he can cease operations…You can have a word now, I'm in his office." Drake handed the phone to McDonald who made no move to accept it. Drake placed the phone back at his own ear, "Seems he doesn't want to have that conversation right now…Right."

Drake hung up and gave McDonald a smug sneer. "I'll expect my money by tomorrow."

"Drop dead."

"And risk another inquest delay?" Drake chortled as he strolled from the office.

The phone on McDonald's desk rang instantly. McDonald put out a steady hand to answer it. "Yes? … Agreed." He replaced the handset contentedly.

Cecil sat at his government issued desk in the Homicide Division of the Metropolitan Police shuffling half a dozen faded file folders. The office was all guts no glory, inexpensively furnished and neatly organized. An empty cardboard file box sat just to his left. It was marked "Pending: 1996+"

Cecil picked one file at random and began to read. It profiled the unsolved murder of a young Customs and Excise officer at Gatwick Airport in 1996. The cause of death was strangulation by human hands, assumed to have occurred during the robbery of the Customs warehouse at Gatwick. The missing items were reproduction Buddha statues from Thailand. He closed that file and moved on to another. File #2 revealed the unsolved murder of six Chinese stowaways on a cargo ship from Shanghai in 1998. The ship was carrying reproduction Terracotta Warriors from China. One pallet was missing from the lading order, but no insurance was ever claimed by the consignee or the shipper. File #3: the murder of a FedEx courier en-route to deliver a small shipment of six sacred stones from Indonesia. Three stones were stolen and never recovered. The remaining three stones were determined to be fakes. File #4: a museum guard gunned down near a storage room housing gift shop surplus. The only item missing was a small box of reproduction Kashmiri scarabs. Cecil closed the files with disgust and replaced them in the Pending box, picking up a pen to fiddle with, more nervous habit than constructive energy. Also on his desk was the Hathaway file. He noted in a corner "wanted by ESCU" on it as the phone rang. He answered on the first ring. "Cecil."

"Hello. It's Matthew Stephens Gilbert."

"Found your client yet?" asked Cecil feigning boredom while his heart raced.

"Yes. That's why I'm calling."

Cecil hit a button on the phone that began a trace request for the phone's location, the caller ID already noting the number from which the call emanated. "Bring her in. I'll be here."

"She won't come. I don't want her to run again."

"Convince her it's for her own good."

"I'm not so sure. Someone's been shooting at us. She wants to stay hidden."

"For fuck's sake!" Cecil yelled all pretence abandoned. "All the more reason to come in. We can protect her."

"From whom?" Matt wondered aloud.

"Whoever's after her."

"That's just it. Only you and Sussex want her. Of course they could have been shooting at me."

"Then she's safer with me. And you're safer too. I won't charge you with impeding an investigation. Look. There's a warrant for her arrest and I'm off to search her house for a murder weapon."

"What murder?" asked Matt, his attention piqued, "When?

"Johnny Hathaway. At her flat. Yesterday afternoon."

"He was -?" Matt did the math, "It couldn't have been her. She was in custody yesterday. I was there with her. What was--"

"Time," I interrupted.

"Then she has nothing to fear," raced Cecil, knowing Matt was about to hang up and not yet achieving the trace. “An air tight alibi. I still want to speak with her. Maybe she can help.”

“I’ll do my best,” said Matt sincerely as he hung up the phone abruptly.

Cecil just sat staring at the phone. Without realizing he had doodled a gun and the words “repro” and “customs” on his notepad. He looked at it confused. He had no time to ponder his subconscious creation; he had to get back to Lola’s flat before the science boys and girls packed up.

When he entered the trashed apartment, Cecil was struck again by just how violent and painful Hathaway’s death must have been and the same for the struggle that precipitated that demise. Johnny Hathaway was murdered and Cecil wanted, needed, to find his killer before the papers got hold of the details. He walked through the flat scanning the scene and imagining the events in his mind’s eye. A crime scene team had already gathered, bagged and tagged evidence: a full unopened bottle of Cuervo Gold; a smashed bottle of Cuervo Gold; a smashed bottle of Mezcal. There was little left of probative value. He continued to walk just looking not touching. He lingered at the repro artefacts: there was a Thai Buddha head in the living room bookcase and a mini terracotta warrior on the bedside table in the bedroom.

“Hey,” Cecil shouted at one of the techies, “Get a shot of this and that.” He indicated both artefacts.

“The warrant says tequila and bleach,” worried the technician. “We were lucky to get a second bite of the apple. Let’s not screw it up.”

"Humour me," replied Cecil humourlessly. "I'm an art lover."

"On your head be it," conceded the SOCO as he collected the items.

A suited detective rushed in and spoke to Cecil, "Gov, we have a fix. We'd better hurry or we'll lose her…"

Matt hung up the pay phone in the ornate entryway of Harrods department store in Knightsbridge; I was by his side, peering at him nervously.

"What now?" I asked.

"We blend. And wait"

In stark contrast to Cecil's gritty, functional office, Walker' office was all glory. The walls and surfaces were adorned with citations, awards and photographs with politicians including Tony Blair, Gordon Brown and a woman in a dark suit whose face was just out of shot. The furniture was upscale utilitarian.

Walker had been a hunter since his father put a pellet gun in his hands at the age of five. He hunted rabbits, deer and foxes, without the aid of sniffer dogs like those pansies in their red frock coats on silly white horses. He loved the intermingled scents of gun oil, cordite and the metallic iron rich blood of his kill. It energized him more than any other stimulant, natural or synthesized. His adrenaline-pumped heart, already beating furiously from the chase, increased in the exact increment that his prey's heart slowed until it stopped altogether and Walker' heart ripped at his chest as if it wanted to burst free. He felt naked without the black and blue bruises on his upper arm from the rifle's kick and became restless whenever he watched them fade to green and yellow before disappearing altogether.

The culling of rabbits, deer, fox and other vermin were a right bestowed upon him as the son of a landowner to keep the country side safe and prosperous. It made little difference to him if his family ate his catch or not; the killing was his goal in and of itself. Occasionally he would track down an animal sniped from forty feet and find that it had limped back to its den or that its offspring would mew and lick the parent's wounds. Walker swelled with the eradication of an entire family knowing they would never be able to mature and breed, further infesting his land. It was a sign that his goal was worthy and his path true.

As his body grew his need for larger prey increased. Walker' hunt lust escalated until Britain no longer held a sufficient challenge. Instead of college Walker hopped a flight to South Africa with only the clothes on his back and his new sharp shooter, a graduation gift from his father. His mother looked on mutely as she always had when he walked away armed. He never bothered to ask how she felt, not really caring but also knowing that she was resolutely English and did not discuss her feelings or show her emotions. She was neither tactile nor effusive whether he did something right or something wrong. His father however, was very tactile. Easy to reach out with a slap on the back or a tanning of his hide. He had felt the sting of his father's leather belt on his backside only twice before he learned how to achieve just enough to remain invisible or be discreet enough to hide a perceived failing. Walker developed into a crack shot as much from his own desire to kill as from his need to avoid the belt for wasting ammunition. He spent two years in Africa walking north alone with just a compass, killing anything and everything that had the misfortune to step in his path. Never bothering to learn the laws of the land or even caring which borders he had crossed he occasionally had to shoot a ranger intent on curbing his quest for larger and more ferocious prey. Everything that fell to his gun he left after eating his fill, as a gift back to the land that provided his bounty in the safe knowledge that the land would reclaim its own. He hunted for himself and needed no trophies to display or to kindle his memory. While he remembered each kill down to the sinews of his frame, the pleasure dwindled as his prowess grew. By the time he reached Egypt he realized it was time to leave Africa.

He had no desire to return home to his parents. It never even occurred to him to write or call them in his two year sojourn. What then would he have to say to them in person? Nor did he have any desire to return to the countryside, knowing that it housed only tiny creatures unworthy of his skill. It eventually occurred to him on the long train ride through Europe that the killing of the rangers gave him the most heightened rush because it was unplanned, pure instinct. He was smart enough to know that he couldn't pursue that feeling in a nation as civilized as Britain without authority and sanction. By the time he glimpsed the white cliffs of Dover again, he made up his mind to offer his services to anyone who'd let him pack a gun.

The police were largely unarmed and therefore not suitable. MI-5 rejected him after his long form application. The army rejected him after his medical interview even though he was in prime physical fitness. Finally, he was accepted by ESCU, a police investigation division that was just outside of normal policing. The strength of his shooting scores were paramount in their decision because even though it was Britain and the police didn't usually carry guns, the smugglers always did.

At the present moment, however, he felt more like an animal, trapped in the small government office. Restrained when he should be out hunting for vermin that were a plight on society. He hated when his investigations ended in capture and trial and he made a mental note to pack additional ammo when he finally got a lead on Lola Steele.

Matt and I sat in the opulent room that occupied half of the 4th floor of Harrods. Gold and green velvet chairs flanked cream damask tables set with bone china bearing the Harrods logo. In the centre of the room sat a majestic five tiered, 15-foot-long table displaying hundreds of cream cakes, cookies, cakes, scones, finger sandwiches, pastries and delectables of every type and variety. My mind had already photographed the gleaming chocolate frosting on the eclairs, the glistening apricot glaze on the fruit tarts and the soldier like rows of pastel macarons. It had framed dozens of shots for a cookbook that would never be written. The scene rivalled Willy Wonka's chocolate room – even surpassed it for the well-heeled Chanel set of Knightsbridge. Crisply dressed waiters in starchy white shirts and long aprons over black tuxedo trousers with matching black bow ties wielded silver teapots like medicinal urns. The room heaved with tourists and tea connoisseurs. There was also a long line waiting at the door. Matt and I sat at a small table in the back, me hidden from the front entrance by the buffet itself. Matt had just enough of a view to monitor who came and went, which he did with an occasional, seemingly indifferent gaze. Only Matt went to the buffet to refill our plates.

For the first time in hours, I managed a wee smile, "I am in heaven thank you. But unless it's a 24 hour buffet, we need a plan."

"I'm working on it. You know this place is for tourists. No self-respecting Englishman would have tea this way."

"Nor those without self-respect. I'm counting on it," I mumbled, my speech obstructed by a jammy creamed scone.

Unbeknownst to me, my calorific orgy was in jeopardy as DCI Cecil and his colleague arrived at the Hans Crescent entrance to the store. In fact, each entrance was flanked by uniformed officers of the Metropolitan Police. As he exited his unmarked vehicle, Cecil held a device to his lips and began to address the comms system clipped to each of their right shoulders. "Nobody lets her leave. But nobody causes a panic. We don't want to cause any grief for the store's proprietor." Mostly Cecil didn't want to be hauled into his superintendent's office to answer complaints that would surely follow if Mr.

Fayed's business was caused any more grief by Her Majesty's agents.

Instructions delivered, Cecil pocketed his radio and signalled to the younger detective. They entered the store and began a meticulous, floor by floor search. He didn't really expect to find Lola shopping and was careful to include changing rooms, lavatories and ornate stairwells in the search. At the conclusion of each floor, Cecil radioed his sentries to confirm that Lola had not exited the premises. It took approximately 18 minutes to scour each level, less for mezzanines and restaurants. Just over an hour after they began, Cecil arrived at the Georgian Restaurant on the fourth floor. He was able to walk straight up to the Maître d' as the line had dissipated, all the thirsty travellers neatly dispatched to linen havens. As he spoke his eyes roamed the interior. He was distracted from the anonymous faces by the large buffet table; although it was one third the size of its former self having been consolidated as teatime drew to a close, it was still impressive to a hungry plodding police officer.

My hunger had been sated 15 minutes ago and the lack of distraction let my mind slip back to my predicament. "Still working on your plan?" I asked Matt.

"Keep eating," he instructed distantly.

"I can't," I said, a worry forming as I watched his face.

"The store closes in 15 minutes. We have to get the car out or we're immobile. Or highly visible."

"Well that's a plan…of sorts," I conceded.

The niggling doubt solidified as Matt eyed the entrance for the 200th time; he noticed Cecil's approach as he neared the entrance, and leaned subtly to his right so he too was somewhat hidden by the buffet. He raised the gleaming silver teapot and studied the reflection as Cecil began his chat at the front of house. Matt gently placed his hand on mine and said, "Time to go." He placed a £50 note on the table and rose slowly. I did likewise.

We quickly but discretely headed to the back stairwell by the toilets without being noticed.

As the heavy mahogany door closed behind us, the Maitre d' was studying a photo of me. He turned and scanned the room, finally pointing to the empty table Matt and I previously occupied. Cecil closed in and examined the remains on the table noting that the large bank note was still there and figuring that if a waiter hadn't had time to swing by and collect the princely sum, it hadn't been left that long ago. Which meant that I was still here, somewhere. He pulled out his walkie-talkie again and spread the word, "She's still here, probably heading towards an exit. High alert gentlemen."

Matt and I descended the grey nondescript stairwell which starkly contrasted the grandeur of the dining room.

"So much for the high life," I murmured.

"You did it again!" whispered Matt.

"I did?"

"The high life. Any VIP room – plenty of drugs, never a cop in sight. You can get into VIP rooms right?"

"Usually. But today has not been usual."

"What's our best bet?"

"To get in or to get lost in the crowd?!

"Both."

"The Bond Club."

"Good! Valet parking right?"

"That's right! You pull up to the door, I run inside, sign us in; the valet will come out and take the keys from you. No offence but you won't be recognized. Only give the keys to the guy with the black polo top who comes out of the door I go in. Anyone else will keep the car."

"Ha ha. Even if I am recognized, I'm not the one they want."

"So you're sure now it's me they're shooting at? I need to make a call."

"Pay phone. Not here though."

Matt and I entered the underground parking garage through what turned out to be the workers' entrance to/from the car park. We saw the uniformed police officers searching, stopping at every black Jeep Wrangler and silver BMW and checking the license plates. I ducked down instinctively and Matt followed suit. We duck walked to the little red Porsche and entered it quietly. I crouched down in the foot well doing my best pretzel impersonation. Matt drove out casually, watching the policemen peripherally.

A stack of ammo boxes neatly piled on his desk, Walker relaxed in his office with his polished brogues on the waxed desktop, smoking a Cuban cigar and feeling pleased with himself. Until Cecil entered without knocking.

"Raised in a barn?" scowled Walker at his intruder.

"I need to view the items confiscated from the Steele raid," stated Cecil without preamble or small talk.

"No can do. Chain of evidence you know." Walker liked being obstructive.

"Will be preserved you know." Cecil hated obstructionists.

The phone on his desk rang before Walker could reply to Cecil. He snatched the handset, changing his posture only slightly until he was forced to sit up abruptly. His expression changed from pleased to angry. He listened to what was clearly a tirade, scratchy high pitched noises leaking from the phone. At the first hint of pause Walker jumped in, "Not my fault. Not my problem," he barked.

The noises at the other end of the line took on a more sinister pitch and Walker's anger grew into red faced fury. Cecil did not even pretend discretion, pulling a chair close to the desk and resting his elbows on the polished wood and his gaze on Walker' face. Walker gestured wildly for Cecil to leave but Cecil was enjoying the moment too much. To play with Walker, Cecil stood, stretched and ambled over to the wall of glory to study the photos. When Cecil's eyes lingered on a signed band photo, and then a group of politicians, Walker' agitation reached peak levels.

His tone into the phone turned malevolent, "We are stuck with each other mate!" The "mate" brought more shrill screaming and a slam on the other end. As he replaced the handset in its cradle, Walker resettled the smug expression back onto his face and addressed Cecil, "You were begging?"

"Do you need to attend to something?" inquired Cecil casually, "He clearly wasn't happy with your performance."

"Men are seldom happy. Was there anything else before you left?"

"I want to see Lola Steele's effects," demanded Cecil, all pretence of request forgotten.

"That request was already denied."

"It wasn't a request."

"Then that statement was ignored. Now, will you be leaving voluntarily?"

"What are you hiding? Have you screwed up the chain already? Accidental or tampering? How long will you need to fudge it? I'm free tomorrow too."

"You're leaving now. Door or window?" Walker's tone matched the severity of his threat. He stood up to his full six foot five inch height.

Cecil just smiled, "Until tomorrow then."

The photos in Walker' office gave Cecil the germ of an idea, but it caused a dilemma. If he was right, and he did nothing, all the evidence would be destroyed. If he was wrong, he could embarrass himself and hinder his chances of a promotion in the near future. At 38 he didn't have much longer to advance his career. Not that he relished a more administrative position, but his eye was on the prize and the prize was a big, fat pension in twenty more years. If he was right and he agitated the situation, he would start a landslide of aggravation and manipulation that would challenge him to the core, and could result in a target on the back of his own head.

He decided to go for it, figuring that oysters only produced pearls if they were irritated by an unwelcome grain of sand.

The law firm of Stephens Gilbert & Co., usually referred to as SG & Co., occupied a venerable brownstone on St. John's Place in Farringdon. The neighbourhood was populated by small office buildings alongside cafes, restaurants, bars, pubs and clubs. The area was in full swing night life, but the office buildings were dark, except the top floor where Matt and his partners plied their trade. All the windows were brightly lit as were the purple hued spotlights on the roof from the tech teams searching every nook and cranny. Matt's new 'cleaning company' was carrying out technical surveillance counter measures.

They were dressed as sleek cleaning crew but their actions were slightly off kilter for mere dusting and vacuuming. They swept with a radiofrequency detector to scan for transmitters by moving the instrument slowly and methodically around the spaces. The RfD had a range of 10hz – 24hz and made a pinging sound that got louder as it got closer to audio recording devices. Also in use was a nonlinear junction detector, which sniffed out semiconductor electronics, an infrared scanner, and a visible light emitter to scan for glints from hidden cameras. The last step was a radiofrequency scanner with a wide enough range check for microwaves It had a laser detection mode to find the method of data transmission from the audio and video recorders.

Matt's office was modern, masculine and minimal. In contrast, his partner Jennie Jonasory's was female, antique and accessorized. The other five partners decorated somewhere in between, however all were very professional and well organized. A mobile phone rang and the black boiler suited tech leader, Robin Fry, pulled it from his pocket and answered tersely.

"Speak."

The voice on the other end of the phone belonged to the office's main occupant. Matt asked, "How's my office?"

"Dirty. Very dirty." The cleaners Matt ordered earlier in the day were in fact a top-notch security firm that swept the offices regularly for GSM listening devices, cameras and other unwelcome surveillance bugs planted by Matt's adversaries from time to time. The main area of practice for Stephens Gilbert, Innocent & Partners was white collar crime. The first time the bugs were traced back to Customs, 242 convictions were overturned when the unauthorized surveillance was discovered. It would have only been Matt's single client had he discovered the listening device earlier during trial, but by the fifth week of its use in situ, and with it being tied to a current sting operation, all 242 persons accused in the campaign across the nation had to be either released or granted appeal. Once it was determined that their convictions may have been obtained on the basis of illegal evidence, the convictions were deemed unsafe and overturned. Those not yet convicted were dismissed with prejudice and the others just not pursued. Six years later it amazed Matt that ESCU were still willing to disband entire operations in the pursuit of privileged information to which they had no right.

The tech leader said, "Sanitising now," hung up and pocketed his phone. Jargon for removal of all devices.

Matt smiled, knowing that any case against Lola would dissipate in light of this, if he lived to tell anyone, let alone present the evidence in open court. He listened, lingering on the pay phone in Chinatown in London's Soho district, as his colleague disconnected with the familiar click. He waited a little longer, phone against his ear, for the second click indicating that the tech's mobile was also tapped, as they both knew it had been for some time now.

I watched contently from the security of the car. I had used the same pay phone previously to alert the club I was bringing a guest, as was the rule. In the open street, I was decidedly nervous feeling very exposed. It was only slightly better in the confines of the car and I was relieved when Matt returned to ferry us to the security of the Bond Club.

The sleek red Boxster crawled along Dean Street. "There," I pointed. "Where?" asked Matt, eying the locked doors and dark windows hidden behind blinds. "The black doors," I replied a hint of superiority escaping. As Matt stopped the car in the middle of the road, blocking the impatient traffic, one of the heavy doors parted and a spry lad sprang out, running to open first my door, and then Matt's. As Matt climbed out, he noticed the boy's outstretched hand and stared at it. "Give him the key," I advised patiently. Matt handed him the key and stepped out of the way as the valet jumped in and raced off. "How do you know he's not a car jacker?" queried Matt.

"I don't," I chided.

I led Matt through the nondescript black door and into the antechamber of one of London's most exclusive private membership clubs. The Bond Club, known only to its members and their guests, accepted membership only from media and entertainment types, and only upon nomination from several members of long standing. There were no application forms. No references. And no requests for membership. If they didn't ask you to join, you couldn't.

The reception area was disappointingly dank for a place of such mystique and renown. A black, semi-circular reception desk shielded a pretty young blond and a stern matronly woman. The leather couch to the right was empty but bore the imprints of guests who arrived early for members who would never arrive timely. Behind the desk was a well lit corridor leading to a coat check room and other doorways. But to the left was the door that Mattered: the big black door with the round window way above my eye level. That was the door to the inner sanctum and the beautiful life.

I ambled up to the desk. "Hello Amber, hello Jean. This is my guest, Matthew Stephens-Gilbert."

"Hello Lola. Good evening sir," smiled Amber. She could as easily have been at an advertising agency or on a photo shoot. She was the cover girl for young Conservative poise and sophistication.

Jean on the other hand was steel. "Mr Stephens-Gilbert I'll need your phone please."

"Um, I don't have one," sputtered Matt.

"Mr Stephen-Gilbert. I'm sure that's not true," persisted Jean, "You could not possibly survive without one."

"That's true," replied Matt finding his feet, "I couldn't normally. But tonight I am without because I left it on the motorway, and am in no mood to go back and retrieve it." He flashed his most disarming grin which failed to move her.

"I was there," I chimed in, "it was actually me who threw it out the window. Don't ask me why," I said cutting off their mental enquiries and grabbing Matt by the elbow. I led him through the door before they could insist on answers.

I led Matt to a sofa against the wall of a softly lit room of beige, orange and brown hues. A long chrome bar adorned the far wall of the long narrow room and each of the dozen bar stools bore the weight of a celebrity bum. Lenny Henry and Lenny Kravitz were drunkenly trying to convince a suited man that "The Two Lenny's" would be a welcome addition to the BBC's fall line-up. In the far left corner James Corden was ticking the leg of Jane Goldman while at the far end of the room Jonathan Ross was pretending to play piano to accompany his un-tuned crooning. Behind him was a steep wide staircase leading to the upper echelons. Matt shook himself out of his star gazing, “Shouldn’t we head to the VIP room? Looks like there are a lot of publicity seekers here.”

“The whole place is a VIP room,” I explained, “the private rooms need to be pre-booked and are for dining or staying overnight. Relax, it’s media and entertainment types only and even they have to be members.”

“Media types? Journalists?” sputtered Matt cynically.

“Some,” I replied my voice a clear indication that there was nothing to worry about.

“But they’ll know you’re wanted,” reminded Matt in a loud whisper.

“Celeb journos, not crime reporters,” I assured.

“I’m not encouraged by their integrity,” worried Matt.

Haughtily I shot back, “The Bond is sacrosanct. Everything stays within these walls. The penalty is membership cancellation; banishment even as a guest.”

Matt couldn’t believe her naiveté, “Ooh. What’s that compared with a career breaking scoop or £10k to someone whose career is on the decline?”

His condescension was unforgivable and I let rip, albeit under my breath, “Blackballed from here is blackballed from the whole industry. No one will touch you if they can’t trust you. It’s why you never read about who was here the night before. The 6am girls tried it once and haven’t been allowed in since. And they were only allowed in then because no one knew who they were personally. Just guests of Pete Docherty – he’s not been back since either. They’ve been trying to make amends since. Poor lambs. Even if they got a tip now, they wouldn’t print it.”

Matt felt sorry for me. "It's the 3am girls honey, I'm sorry but you can't believe everything you hear."

Although he tried to be gentle, the look on my face was twisted. I was holding my emotions in and the strain showed on my face. Finally, when I could control myself no longer, I burst out laughing. "You sad, sweet man. They were the 6am girls on the local sister rag; they were demoted by the publisher for breaking the oath, but promoted to the national for guts. But thank you for trying to be gentle with me. I'm hungry again. How about a burger?"

"In a private dining room?" asked Matt hopefully, grateful for the change of subject to hide his embarrassment.

"Would you chill?!?" I said not accepting his attempt at humour. I got up and walked the two feet to the bar. The bartender, who was just finishing his phone call, came over and took my order.

Josh's houseboat rocked gently on the still Thames. Although inwardly dark, the ambient light of dusk bathed the interior in shadow and light. The silhouettes of the two men caused the boat to rock and belied hurried, nervous movement. Their voices were hushed but hostile.

The final remnants of a setting sun revealed Jake Drake and Rupert McDonald, but no Josh Steele.

"You idiot. You've never been detail oriented. What if he didn't bring it home?" attacked Jake.

"It's not at the office so it must be here," replied Rupert calmly, "The man has no other life."

Unappeased, Jake tore into Rupert again, "Well apparently he does, as it's not here!"

Unruffled, Rupert checked his cuffs and nails, "I propose you keep searching. I have both a dinner date to entertain and an accounting department to take the blame. You, on the other hand, have only a long jail sentence if you don't find it."

"I also have a big mouth," spat an enraged Jake, "I will take you as my cellmate, but you can be someone else's bitch!"

Rupert stopped in his tracks. He took a deep breath and centred himself, "Yes. You would. You're dishonourable and forgetful – losing your own files and interrupting me while Josh had mine." Rupert pulled a small automatic pistol from the pocket of his dinner jacket and shot Jake at point blank range. The houseboat rocked, with intensity this time. "Problem solved," whispered Rupert incongruously after the explosion of the previous moment.

DCI Cecil tested the handle of the rickety door in the unlit, dreary corridor. It was hard to tell if the walls were civil servant grey or law enforcement drab. The offices beyond the other doors were equally dark and no less depressing. But the office behind this door was different as he already knew. A click sounded as the handle depressed further. Cecil stepped into Stuart Walker' office, removing his pick from the lock and quietly closing the door behind him. From his jacket he pulled out a pair of wayfarer sunglasses and slipped them on. The room was plunged into a deeper blackness. Next he pulled out a set of keys and felt his way to the small black pad, similar to a car entry fob. He pressed this button and the infra red was activated on the glasses. Cecil could see the entire room which emanated an eerie cerise glow, only to him. "Eat your heart out Ian Fleming," he whispered to himself. Cecil's search began with a rummaging of Walker' desk, revealing three interesting items: an inventory of the search of Lola's flat; an oddly coded ledger; and a set of keys with a blank identifying tag. Happy with his finds, Cecil pocketed the items and slipped out as quietly as he entered.

Cecil continued his search in the corridor, no longer testing door handles but peering into the rooms themselves. A loud clang echoed through the halls as he walked into a metal bucket, sloshing water onto the floor.

A cranky old man in janitor garb shoved his head out of another door way. "What are you blind?!?" he shouted as he bounded towards Cecil before he stopped abruptly. "Oh geez, I'm sorry sir. Here let me help you," he offered as he saw Cecil wearing sunglass in the dark hallway.

Amused and gracious, Cecil stifled a chuckle, "No need. My apologies. Too much pride to use a stick."

"I completely understand," said the janitor already starting to repeat some Hail Mary's. Matt hurried away, this time with his arms outstretched, feeling in front of him.

"I'm sorry sir, you can't go in there." Jean's formidable voice stopped Stuart Walker in his tracks. "You can't refuse me entry, I'm an officer of the law," postured Walker.

"Your card says East Sussex Customs Unit, not London police. You can make an appointment to see our accountant as per usual," replied the unflappable Jean handing him back his card.

"I'm not an auditor I'm an officer, an investigator!" spat Walker, clearly enunciating his words.

"Then you should have a warrant."

"I have probable cause; I don't need a warrant."

"Of what? Someone isn't going to declare his cocktail? What you need is an invitation or your own membership."

Exasperated, Walker reached into his pocket, "Fine how much to join?"

Two huge burly bouncers appeared behind Walker and in front of The Door as soon as his hand dipped. Jean and Amber stifled a chuckle. "It doesn't work that way. You have to be invited to join. I'm afraid," Jean said with undisguised amusement, "I'll have to ask you to step outside."

Furiously, Walker shoved his wallet back into his pocket and eyed the doormen, before banging into the street doors and storming back into the night and over to the dark Mercedes blocking the street.

Oblivious to the commotion on the other side of The Door, Matt and I stood and approached The Door to the reception area. The bouncers stepped slightly to the side to let us through. Matt took command, “You wait inside until I get the car.”

Still unconvinced we should leave I queried his newfound authority, “And go where?”

“I’d tell you but I’d have to kill you.”

“That line is getting old. You don’t have a plan do you?”

“No.”

“Then drop me at Josh’s. I need a change of clothes.”

“You keep clothes at your ex-husband’s?”

“No, I’ll be borrowing his.”

“Then you can borrow mine. We’ll go to my country house.”

“You have a country house?”

“Yes. And?”

“Nothing. I’m just surprised. I figured you for weekends in Paris, not the countryside.”

Happy to be leaving at any cost, Matt let it slide.

“It’s as good a plan as any,” I agreed, eager to see what kind of country abode attracted the modern city lawyer. We exited the haloed inner sanctum and Matt requested his car. The valet who parked the car appeared from the back room, at a discreet signal from Amber or Jean. As the boy swung through the street doors, Matt recognized Walker just as Walker espied Matt. Walker burst in tackling a frozen Matt.

One of the bouncers jumped on them both. The other bouncer, Abel, grabbed me and hefted me onto his shoulder in a fireman’s carry. He slammed open The Door and rushed through. Running now, he raced to the far end of the room and up that long flight of stairs. I tried to lift my head to see if people were staring but Abel was too fast and all I saw were feet and knees. Jonathan Ross did tinkle an extra ivory, though, so at least one person was aware of the commotion.

The first flight of stairs led to a second that I never knew existed, then a third and finally a grand ballroom on the fourth floor. Abel sprinted to the far corner of the room. We heard shouting and boots thudding up the steps, getting nearer. We were trapped. Abel set me down gently and put his hands against the gilded wall panel with a defeatist, supplicating posture. Panic struck but was interrupted by a small popping sound followed by a low hiss. The panel sprung forward and aside revealing another staircase.

He ushered me in and swung the panel closed behind us. In the dark I could just make out his hand, which moved silently to his lips, signalling for quiet. As our eyes adjusted to the light, the shouts and thuds were upon us. But as quickly as they arrived, the voices and footsteps retreated until they abated altogether. The bouncer took my hand and assured me, “Nobody gets caught at The Bond.”

Abel led me up another flight of stairs within the secret chamber. “That’s why I love it here,” I gushed giddily.

“Up these stairs and onto the roof now,” he instructed.

“What’s up there?” I asked thinking ahead.

“The Churchill Underground,” he explained, “You can cross the rooftops and get down through the Prince Edward Theatre. Then into the street with the theatre crowd.”

“That’s incredible! Is it dangerous? Why the underground?”

“It was a tad dangerous for Churchill because of his limp but you should be fine. It’s a misnomer, a safety device for loose lips during the war. The name just stuck. Follow the rooftops to the Prince Edward on Greek Street. The roof door is always open for us. Good luck honey."

I planted a kiss on his cheek before he slipped back through the door and I started up the stairs.

I thought the Churchill Underground was a myth. Certainly the underground part was. It seemed the elderly, heavy set former Prime Minister was not as lumbering a man as he appeared.

I identified the Prince Edward thanks to an elaborate Victorian sign on the horizon. Studying the varying terrain of the rooftops I calculated that I would have to go south to Old Compton Street's structures then east. In between I was alarmed to see a gap where I'd have to cross Frith Street 30 feet above street level. To abate the rising panic I decided that I would cross that bridge when I came to it, even if I had to build it myself. The roof of the Bond was flat and I was at the edge in three strides. Luckily I was heading east; the facade of the Bond where Walker was brawling with Matt was on the west side. I ran to the edge abutting the next building and was relieved to find its level was a mere two feet lower albeit steepled. I edged over the side of the roof and slid down to the eaves of the next. I then had to scale back up to mount the summit. Scouting around for a handhold upon which to hoist myself, I noticed an old rope. Luck was certainly on my side I thought as I dragged myself up one side and noticed another rope on the other side to rappel myself down. It occurred to me that luck had nothing to do with it! This was Ol' Winston's route. To orient myself to Churchill's escape path I imagined the route through the camera lens of my mind and reduced the photo to a fading sepia tone. Churchill was taller than I was but also older and bulkier. Adjusting my perspective and mental F stop I could see, with a click and a whrr sound effect for each, traversing aids for most of the rooftops: climbing ropes, overhead pipes, hand height railings. It was genius. I now understood why after his predecessors had lost the Empire, Churchill was still able to win the war.

When I reached the last building before Frith Street I saw it. A zip wire! It was invisible from afar and barely discernible up close, but it was there. I tested it to see if it would hold my weight 50 years after its installation. Even with decades of wear, tear and weather it did and without any creaking of the pulleys. I guessed it had been used in the intervening period or at least maintained ready for use. I inhaled a deep breath to quell the fear and took my leap of faith. As I soared through the night sky I tried to memorize each shot for my own internal pictorial. Fear gave momentary way to the glorious feeling of flying. Then I crashed into the Prince Edward sign, falling stunned to the rough tarred surface. It took a minute to clear my head. I heard distant crowd sounds and shouts of "Taxi!" The show was letting out and I realized that if I didn't hurry I wouldn't be able to blend in with the crowd. Locating the roof door, I hurled myself through without a squeak from well oiled hinges and flew down the first two flights of stairs until I found a crowd with which to attach myself.

The glory of flight faded as I exited the theatre. Although I was well ensconced in a crowd I felt vulnerable to the unknown eyes around me. The crowd veered toward Cambridge Circus and I allowed myself to be swept with it, pulling away towards Covent Garden to join another group. I employed the same technique through Charing Cross and down to the Embankment where I found a nearly deserted thoroughfare. It terrified me to be alone. A patrolling policeman turned onto the street but I managed to hide in a shadow until he passed, however it clarified that I was foolishly conspicuous as a woman walking alone in the dark at this late hour.

I crossed under the arches by the Embankment tube station and sprinted for the River Club, a barge moored on the Thames which was just beginning its nocturnal amusements. Bill, my old mate, was on the door and happy to see me. "All right love?" he hailed as I climbed the gangplank.

"Permission to come aboard Captain?" I saluted.

"Permission granted Miss. Entrance fee."

I walked up and kissed his cheek. He grabbed me and embraced me warmly.

"You alright duck?" inquired Bill.

"Stressful night Bill my son. The world has gone mad." It always amused me that I turned cockney in his presence.

"Yours always does pet. Now why is that? And why is JeepGirl jeep-less?" A doorman's powers of observation and deduction were his stock in trade.

"Long story. Too long."

Bill decided not to pry. With a final squeeze of my hand, he opened the door and bade me a gallant entry.

The club was sparsely inhabited inside, the approach to midnight being too early for serious clubbing. Fear niggled again as I heard the distant wail of sirens growing in hurried decibels. Alarmed I backed towards the rear of the barge away from the door. The barge had its own pier for patrons arriving by the river. I managed a wave and a shaky smile to the bartender on my way. There was only one set of keys on the board beaconing in the moonlight and symbolizing the catalyst of an idea. Just past the board sat a very bored Tim, who "valet" parked the boats, his only charge a small speed boat undulating with the tide of the Thames. "Evening Tim," I chimed.

"Hello love. How you been?" Tim's Welsh sing-songy inflection always tickled me.

"Better. I've been better." My smile was incongruous to my reply; I've always found that people listen to either the tone or the words, choosing the one they want to hear. Tonight Tim chose to go with the smile and breezy tone. I glanced at the board and Tim followed my gaze. "Slow night?"

"Mostly landlubbers," he said, clearly disappointed.

"Not your type at all me hearty."

"Argh." Tim scrunched his face into a one-eyed pirate.

"I think Bill was gesturing for me to get you," I lied. "Not sure. You want to check it out?"

"Why not? Nothing happening here. Keep an eye out 'til I get back?"

I nodded affirmatively but said, "I'm so sorry," very, very sincerely.

"No need, Lola," chimed Tim as he loped off towards the front of house.

Oh yes there is, I thought to myself, as I grabbed the keys without hesitation, untied the speed boat and jumped in. It started without hesitation and I eased it out of the slip heading west. At the last minute I flung my credit card back onto the dock hoping there was enough credit to pay for the "rental."

"LOLA!" shouted Tim when he heard the engine rumble to life "What are you doing?!?"

Truthfully I had no idea. In my fear to not be apprehended I committed my first real crime. Stupid, stupid girl I thought to myself. I knew the club would have a fiduciary duty to call the police and identify me as a thief. It was an expensive item I had just stolen and I had become the very thing I denied yesterday. Or was it the day before. I had no perception of time or space, only motion. I consoled myself that I would return the boat and send a cheque from my new fortune for anything the credit card didn't cover; restitution and bribery would hopefully go a long way to getting them to drop the charges. Easing up through the gears I finally pushed the little junket to full throttle about ten miles downriver. But the engine roar was soon harmonized with a siren. Over my shoulder I glimpsed a police cruiser, lights blazing. I held my course, sympathizing with Thelma and Louise when they realized they had no future, no happy ending. Tears stung my eyes and a black cloud obscured my reason. I turned and raised my hands in surrender, but when I saw the shotguns pointed at me, instinct overrode remorse and depression, and I turned back toward the wheel.

"Cut your engines and prepare to be boarded," shouted a tinny amplified voice.

"Shit, shit, shit" I wailed as I held my course.

"Stop or we'll shoot" bellowed the tannoy drone.

I jerked the wheel sharply just as a shot rang across where my bough had been; at least they weren't trying to kill me, yet.

"That was a warning shot. I repeat, cut your engines and prepare to be boarded."

An idea came as familiarity of the terrain set in. Around the next bend was Josh's houseboat. I set a course to broadside it and killed the engines as instructed. If I could drift there before being boarded by the Thames River Police I could jump ship to ship to shore and make a run for it. If I could just get close enough to jump over, I could get inside and out onto the street. Maybe even get his motorbike on the way; in my mind a photo of the bike whirred. I think I even believed that the keys might be sitting on the seat waiting for me. The reality was that the police boat was gaining on me.

"Turn around and keep your hands raised."

I turned to face my pursuers but sidled toward the port side and the houseboat, arms raised.

"Stand still please."

Resisting arrest would be added to my list of actual crimes but jumping ship was a better idea than jumping the Grand Canyon. It was going to be close. I was nearly alongside Josh's boat but they were closing fast and they were certainly close enough to shoot me in the back when I made my leap to freedom –BOOM!!! My boat knocked into Josh's. Sweat trickled down my back outlining and defining a perfect target on my shirt.

My thought was interrupted a nanosecond later by another deafening noise. The air vibrated and pushed at me, knocking me somewhere, a blinding white light and another flight in the cold night air, this one inglorious as it probably meant I had been shot and was dead. I pondered the lack of pain when an incongruous chill enveloped me, plunging me into darkness and confusion. I couldn't breathe. I felt like a silver marble in a pinball machine, being hit by flippers and propelled hither and yon, but in slow motion. My predominant thought however was that I couldn't breathe! Panic, fear, bewilderment collided in my conscience before reason took over: why did I need to breathe if I was dead? Mystification was dissolving into understanding. I was alive, barely, but drowning, approaching the demise that I erroneously imagined. Awareness became the catalyst for action and I kicked out. As I neared the surface I kicked harder, survival becoming the paramount thought. I broke the surface and gulped the beautiful, polluted but welcome air. Casting a glance about to orient myself, I was giddy to find that I had been flung south away from Josh's mooring on the northern bank. The police cruiser was gone, replaced by burning wreckage much further east. I said a small prayer to God that no one was hurt and was slammed by the realization that Josh would have been killed in the explosion. Anguish reclaimed my soul and I ceased flotation movements. I sank like debris and welcomed the oncoming oblivion, but like all of my late plans, peace didn't come, only more sorrow and frustration at not being able to sob properly. The darkness was like a screen on which to replay the explosion, this time spewing pieces of Josh's body with boat debris. I began to rise, as people float naturally. Angrily I kicked out again and reached for the southern embankment. I wasn't sure where I was but I knew that the southwest was away from the sirens and mayhem approaching the northeast of the river. I cast about for a ladder or handhold to climb ashore but felt only the slimy flat surfaces of the artificial embankment. I felt doomed, another obstacle abruptly halting my shaky resolve.

I tried to emulate the stern tone my mother would use whenever I was feeling sorry for myself, "Focus. Find the hurt and the danger and move away!"

Just as I did as a child with my mother, I tried to argue with myself, "Tired. Cold. Josh. I'm so sorry." But my mother's will was strong, the supportive encouragement firmly implanted on the surface of my conscience, "No! Don't give up. Not your time."

"Mom it's just softball," I whined. "No Lola, it's life," my mother countered sharply, "Today life is about softball and about being able to use the public field, public being the operative word. Tomorrow it might be about being able to go to the local school. In ten years it might be about your freedom. The issue is irrelevant. What's paramount is right and wrong. Right is right and wrong is wrong. It's wrong that your team can't use the mowed baseball fields because the boys' teams have them booked solid and you can't use the other fields because the city won't mow them. You have a right to use the public fields. It is wrong that you are being denied that right." "But Mom, I'm nine and you're a housewife. We can't fight City Hall." I was trying to be reasonable now even though I was furious before when the league said that our team, St. Ann's, had to forfeit because we lost our field to the boys for an unexpected playoff. They'd never qualified for the play off before so an extra game had never been scheduled for them. It was great for them, but it meant that our forfeit would knock us out of the qualifiers. It was very unfair of the park administrators to say that the boys' win was more important than ours. They didn't even try to phrase it fairly. They actually said, "It's great that you want to play your little game of softball but baseball is important." We were crowded around BethAnn, our coach, and I could see her fists balling even though she stood stock still. Now I knew she had a mouth on her and could curse like a sailor, but she didn't say a word just then. I think that infuriated me even more. It almost felt like a double betrayal. That must have been what made me lash out; before I knew I had done it, I broke through the team and stood beside BethAnn my fists clenched too, one shaking in the air as I ranted, "It's discrimination and it's unconstitutional. You may think you have the right to schedule the fields but you certainly don't have the right to base your decisions on gender." He just stared at me stunned for half a second and then started laughing. I know the words were incongruous with my childlike voice but I was deadly serious and it humiliated me to be laughed at. I started crying, really crying. BethAnn put her arm around me until I stopped shaking and the girls all patted me as best they could reach. While they were doing it though, their sense of injustice must have swollen because the next thing I knew, they were trashing his office. BethAnn finally found her voice when the cops arrived, "You can press charges, shithead but I promise you it will become a federal case because of our constitutional rights. I'm sure the Daily News would love that!" I was sure that BethAnn had no more than a passing acquaintance with the Constitution and didn't know anyone at the Daily News but the way the park guy cringed I knew it was a good bluff. I was completely calm by the time the police officer rang the bell to our apartmetn that evening. Even so the look on my mother's face when she opened the door was one of grave concern. "Schtoonk, are you okay?" she asked as she grabbed me and pulled me close. Although I wasn't overly enamoured of that nickname I was gobsmacked that my mother automatically assumed that the police presence was merited by someone else's bad actions and that it never occurred to her I could be in the wrong. "I'm fine Mommy," I assured her. When the officer left I explained what had happened, even the embarrassing bits. That's when she suggested that we take the case to our local representatives: Councillors first, Senators second, Congressman third and finally, if we had to, to the Mayor. That sounded like a long process to me, one that would take us into the next three softball seasons. The point would be moot by then. Suddenly I stopped caring, consoling myself that I could have my afternoons and weekends back and maybe lie on the couch and watch TV again. That's when I said, "It's only softball."

We spent the next five weeks mailing and calling all the local politicians and media. At first it was just me and my mother at our dining room table. By week three there were 25 of us packed into the living room and on the first day of the sixth week there were 127 of us standing on the steps of City Hall and 54 journalists from New York City's biggest newspapers and TV stations on the sidelines. After just 36 minutes of peaceful protest, the mayor himself came out and announced that additional funds would be allocated to our park so that the six additional ball fields could be mowed and maintained for the exclusive use of our softball league. Amidst the whooping and cheering my mother scooped me up as if I were still five and held me as tight as she would if I had been kidnapped and returned home. She was shaking and crying. She let me go just enough to look me in the face and whisper, "Never be afraid to change the world, even if it's just your little world."

"Think Lola think! Change your little world. Take stock. Fire. North. Me. South. So left. East. London. London bad. Go west young man." The child like giggle that ensued indicated I was close to delirium. "No!" I berated myself, "Go! West. West. Barnes. Pier. Yes! Ok. This way. Go. Keep going." I had always been goal oriented and having a plan seemed to settle my erratic ramblings. I was still frightened but rational enough to recall my dentist song, the song I sang silently to calm my nerves in the dentist's chair. It was a show stopper from Les Miserables. I began to sing in a soft whisper, just for the company, "do you hear the people sing, singing the songs of angry men. It is the music of a people who will not be slaves again. When the beating of your heart, echoes the beating of the drum, there is a life about to start when tomorrow comes." It was an effective choice for the dentist because I couldn't always remember the lyrics and I had to concentrate very hard to recall them, thus distracting me from the pain of the drill. My singing faltered now, at the part it always did. I also found I was out of breath and tiring rapidly. In my mind the rational thought was to stop singing and swim which would enable me to reach my destination more quickly. I pushed away and tried to swim. I kicked out from the siding but was so tired that I sunk immediately. As I plunged underwater a spot light swept over the embankment and the river. I could see the bright spot undulate above me. A delusional welcoming beckoned me as I assumed a vague notion that I was supposed to follow the light as I must surely now be dead and approaching heaven. I kicked under water and rose to greet the light, but as I neared, it swept right in a huge arc too fast for me to follow. Panic resumed and I thrashed my way back to the side, my greatest fear being that I could no longer trust my own mind. It had finally dawned on me that it was a menacing search light rather than a friendly lifesaving beam and I recalled in a rush the events leading to my predicament. Once again I reached for my song to allay the fear and keep all other thoughts at bay until I was clear of the water. "Do you hear the people sing? Singing the songs of angry men." Once again I propelled myself, hand over hand along the mossy planks focusing only on lyrics and positional progress.

Eventually I came to an eroded wooden ladder and pulled myself up with the last of my strength. Relief gave way to hysterical sobbing until I was foetal and spent, in a pool of filthy river sludge. Spasms erupted from my gut and a malodorous stream spewed from my mouth. The lingering taste was vile; it became the impetus for renewed vigour.

Once again I was running but this time from myself rather than from any unseen enemy. Basic instinct reasoned that good tastes came from kitchens yet bad smells were often ignored like when five kilos of fish needed gutting and their carcasses simmering with strong onions and lashings of garlic. I thought that maybe my nearly putrid state would be overlooked in the bowels of a prep room at least long enough to swipe some dry clothes and a bottle of water. It wasn't a coherent thought because I was still dripping wet from head to toe, but I couldn't let any rationality derail my momentum.

Barnes wasn't like Kensington and Chelsea where kitchens had rear entrances and basements. Each building abutted the next one as if jostling for its permanence on the space time continuum, but knowing that their lifeline was limited as restaurants came in and out of favour. Sci fi morbidity was not usually my mode of consciousness and by the time I could curtail such randomness I was in a residential area without any hope of chef whites and water. There was still hope of detached houses eventually, a back garden and a clothesline with forgotten washing at least.

It took ten minutes before I found anything suitable if not anywhere near stylish. Desperation draped me in a floral frock and complementary cardigan and I wondered if in a different life someone could have thought me beautiful dressed like this, more Cath Kidston than Camden Lock. I hung my own sodden clothes on the line in their place as part exchange ignoring the knowledge that it would have been kinder to leave them in the bin. I traded my smelly Doc Marten's for soiled beige Timberland work boots a size too large that had been left on the back doorstep. While they didn't smell much sweeter, they were dry. When my boots dried they would be a much better wear than the boots that were departing on my feet and I felt that the bargain struck silently, had come out even if I ignored the size difference.

All I had to find now was a place to bed for the night in an area as alien to me as the jungle would have been. I wondered if that would save me, because no one would think to look for me in a place where I had no links or history.

Matt had spent the intervening period in combat with Walker. Once their physical tussle had been halted, they remained rooted to the spot arguing who would see the other one in jail. The Bond ladies had phoned the police, who had arrived in record time, hoping to find Graham Norton fighting Alan Carr rather than two stiff, suited nobodies. They pulled the men apart only to be bombarded with shouting and threats.

Matt wanted Walker arrested for actual bodily harm evidenced by a bloody gash on Matt's right cheekbone.

Walker wanted to arrest Matt for obstruction of justice and abetting a fugitive.

The Met Police however, wouldn't release Matt to Walker once Matt handed over Cecil's card.

The disappointed and harried Bobbies decided that they could either arrest both for their public melee or release both if they promised to go separate ways. Walker didn't even deign to verbalise his option but merely stormed off to the waiting Mercedes.

Matt watched him depart and continued to watch as the rear door opened for Walker before he even reached the vehicle. Matt was taken aback by the thought that a passenger in a government vehicle observed the spectacle but refrained from interfering with or aborting it. Why? The answer to that question would likely lead to a string of more answers, tumbling the mysteries like a mile of dominoes. He recalled Cecil's frustration at thinking ESCU a law unto themselves and he now knew that Cecil was absolutely correct.

As if on cue now that Dean Street was cleared of obstructing vehicles from the world of law enforcement, the valet pulled gently in front of the club. He left the engine running as he exited the car and handed the keys to Matt. "How bad does the other guy look?" queried the car courier as he dashed back into the club, not waiting for an answer or a tip.

Matt was disappointed to think that Walker probably wasn't marked at all.

Matt drove the Porsche as quietly as possible to the leafy street in Notting Hill where he lived in an old Victorian Terrace in need of much TLC. He cruised slowly searching for a parking spot when he noticed Josh Steele sitting on his front steps, loitering, clutching papers to his chest and struggling to stay awake. Matt carried on past the house, still searching and finally found a parking spot on the street further down. Matt walked back to his house and confronted Josh, "You ok? … Josh?"

Josh was groggy as if he'd been sleeping with his eyes open. He stood up as he replied, "Yeah. Matt. Thanks. Goodness, where have you been? What happened to your face? Scratch all that. Can I come in?"

Matt wanted to go in just as much so he said, "Sure," and unlocked the door ushering Josh inside and scanning the street before closing the door behind himself.

Inside, Matt's home had the look of a place decorated by a stylish woman a while ago and not kept up since. It was neat and tidy; masculine bits had been added and seemed off kilter. A sleek black leather recliner sat next to a damask sofa and arm chair. Wicker baskets, plants and candles had been piled into a corner of the living room alongside a box with hastily discarded knick-knacks. The varied surfaces of the brown furniture were bare save for some law books and men's magazines.

Matt led Josh to the barely used kitchen and extracted two bottles of beer from the nearly empty fridge. Handing one to Josh Matt asked, "What's going on?"

Josh hung his head ashamedly, "I didn't know who to turn to. Your phone is off. Your office didn't know where you were. Johnny is missing. Ditto Lola. There are police at her flat. Johnny's house is empty. What the fuck Matt?"

Matt smiled because he had wanted to phrase his query the same way but years of legal argument had beaten the swears out of his speech, if not his thoughts. "I'm not sure. You're a mess. What happened to you?"

"So are you," smiled Josh in return. "Where to begin? At the beginning I guess."

"Is this a long story. Will we need more drinks?

Josh nodded affirmatively but said, "No. yes. Short story. Still need more drinks." Matt grabbed two more bottles and led Josh to an iron patio table with two wrought iron chairs at the end of the room in what would have been a dining room if it had a larger indoor table and more seating.

Josh took a long pull from his opened bottle and began, "Right. I was auditing Zulu Records for Johnny. Routine annual audit, do it every year or so. I usually recover a shortfall of quarter million – no big deal. This time. No short fall. Some curious overpayments, though. I query them but the documents I receive aren't just for Johnny. They're for other artists too – but in the same territory. Which is probably where the confusion started but--"

Matt interrupted, "Slow down. I'm not following."

Josh continued, "Albania."

"What about Albania?"

"And Russia. Latvia. Iraq. China. Thailand."

"Yes…?" Matt was impatient but decided to let Josh continue the narrative in his own way.

"Non-copyright countries. All currency controlled. But high royalties being accounted. And goods being purchased in lieu for import to the UK."

"In lieu of what?"

"Money transfers. Cash. You can't send money abroad from there so you buy goods, ship them to the UK, resell them and account for the cash in royalties. Abba started it by buying bananas in the 70's."

"Clever. So what's the problem?"

"There's too much money."

"I wouldn't complain about that."

"For the economies. The populations of these countries could not justify these sales figures. Especially if they're non-copyright signatories. They simply wouldn't import or press that many discs or generate than many downloads. The general populace couldn't afford it. They'd buy pirate copies or get illegal downloads. The documents I have on Johnny alone would mean everyone in Morocco had to buy six copies of the album to justify the figures. And the company used the money to buy Egyptian souvenirs. Why Egyptian souvenirs from Morocco? 30,000 desk top sized and one life sized sarcophagus. Where did they go? Also, the royalty split is weird. 75% to Lola. She should only get 50%. And then 90% of it comes back labelled recoupment. Of the 25% in Johnny's account they also take 90% back in recoupment, leaving what I'd expect from Morocco anyway. Now, if it did that every time, I'd think computer glitch; bad input by accounting. But it's different every time. No matter what, and no matter which band, the bulk of money goes to Lola."

"Our Lola?"

"Yup. Was she a super muse?"

"So that's where it's from. Where did it go?"

"You knew about this? Does Lola know?"

"She does now. We saw her bank statements yesterday."

"She finally opened them? Why yesterday? Is she spending the money? It's what broke us up. She wouldn't use the money herself. She wouldn't let my band have it either. She didn't believe in us."

"If you believed in yourself you wouldn't have needed her money. You'd have got jobs and used your own."

"That's what she said. I get it now. But not back then. I was angry and bitter. So I quit her and the band. I thought she'd relent to save me from the real world and accountancy. I only picked it because she despised it. I was a fool. Anyway. Why yesterday?"

"She didn't open them. Walker from customs had copies."

"Customs? As in HMRC? What do they have to do with this?"

"No, East Sussex police. They have a customs unit at Gatwick. She was arrested by them yesterday and questioned about her account being used to launder money. Can you corroborate that she never opened the statements?"

"Sure. There's still a box of them in storage with the marital property that wasn't important enough to fight over."

"Well they're important now. Where are they?"

"Big Yellow Box. Brighton. Near my parents."

"Who else knows about the place?"

"No one I guess. Except Johnny. Lola gave him a key before we were finally divorced. Just to piss me off I think."

"Sorry mate. More bad news. Johnny's dead."

"Dead? When? How?" Josh was shocked but he didn't break down the way Lola did. It occurred to Matt that the three of them, Lola, Josh and Johnny, had managed to accomplish a spectacular break up by remaining friends and colleagues. He finally understood what was meant by the music industry being incestuous.

"Murdered. Day before yesterday. At Lola's place. The police want to question her too."

"How's she handling it?" Matt just shook his head so Josh pushed thinking the worst, "Where is she? She didn't…"

"No she didn't. I don't know where she is."

"You don't trust me?"

"I really don't know. I lost her in Soho. I got pulled out of the Bond and she got carried inside. She never came back out."

Josh sucked in his breath, "The Churchill Underground. I thought it was a myth. An underground escape passage to avoid the bombs during World War II."

"Where the hell does it go?"

Before Josh could answer the phone rang startling them both. It was way too late for a social call. Matt reluctantly picked it up but hurriedly said, "It's bugged," to a recorded voice asking whether he'd accept the charge of the call from a Stella. He said, "Yes," and as soon as the call connected he again hurriedly uttered, "It's bugged."

Lola's far away voice sounded scared and distraught, "Shit. Oh shit." She was crying.

"Where are you?"

"Can't tell you – bugged. Josh is dead. Bomb. Boat. Dead."

"Babe. Babe. Calm down. Maybe he wasn't home." Matt furiously gestured for Josh to listen with him.

"I can't talk now. I'm coming to get you. Where?"

"I don't know. I'm lost. I can find the King's Head I think. Tomorrow when it's light, no, can't, I'm afraid of the daylight; too conspicuous."

"I know at least three King's Heads."

"Where Livingston played."

"I don't--" Josh gave Matt a thumbs up sign.

"Ok, we'll be there in 20 minutes."

"I can't make it that soon. Tomorrow night. Just after dark."

"Ok but my car is a problem."

"Why?"

"They know it now and, well, you'll see. Stay hidden. You're in danger."

"Ya think?!?! They shot at me again. Police this time. Why?"

"I'll explain later. Stay safe. It's going to be all right."

"Promise?"

"Promise." Matt hung up and turned to Josh, "You'll stay here tonight. Tomorrow we'll go over these accounts, then we'll get Lola. And then, we're goin' to the seaside."

I walked along the deserted street aimlessly. I had to find a place to bed for the night but I had no ideas. Hearing Matt's voice and sharing the burden of Josh's death had a small salve effect but I still felt small and alone, a lost frightened child in the dark. The still of the night was interrupted by an approaching car, its headlights cutting through my isolation with a mix of hope and anxiety. I backed myself into a shadow with a large measure of precaution watching while it crawled to a spot at the curb. The weary driver, in rumpled suit and tie, spilled out and walked away, his right hand reaching back, aiming his key fob at the car. If he clicked the safety lock it wasn't apparent because nothing happened. No lights flashed and no sound beeped. Either the car locked silently and darkly, or he failed to lock the vehicle.

I heard a heavy door close further down the block and realized the man wasn't coming back. I berated myself for not catching him and charming him into letting me stay. Then I chastised myself for thinking I had that kind of charm dry, let alone wet and smelly, or was even that kind of girl. Slowly, I crept out of the shadow and approached the passenger side of the newly parked car. I could see up close that it was a Mini Cooper, not new but not so many years advanced. I held my breath while I tried the door. I lifted the handle and pulled the door open an inch waiting for an alarm to ring. I was prepared to run but it proved unnecessary; the lock had never engaged. Now that I had the door open, I wasn't sure what to do. I slid inside, thinking it was safer to be inside than out, and if I was in the passenger seat, at least it wouldn't look like I was stealing it if anyone came by.

As I sat down on the soft leather seat it enveloped me and I imagined it was a comforting embrace. The warm thoughts brought hot tears to my burning eyes and I realized as I sat how tired I was both physically and mentally. I thought about sleeping but the loss of control from the loss of consciousness frightened me and I began to shake. It didn't feel like a shiver from the cold because my teeth weren't rattling. It was a physiological rebellion, my body telling me it could take no more; even my mind deluded me into wanting more action. I closed my weeping eyes and sang softly to myself again, this time a ballad from the same musical, something about giving up hope, the only line I remembered in its entirety, “Life has killed the dream I dream.” Finally I let myself slumber, no longer caring what happened.

Today, Part 2

When I woke to the singing of birds it was still dark in the direction I faced but I sensed warmth at my back where the sun was rising in the east. I could see lights being switched on in houses as people awoke to a new day. Quickly I climbed out of the Mini and closed the door quietly. I must have slept soundly in the same position because my muscles atrophied. I was very stiff and achy. I wasn't sure if my unpaid motel for the night added to my list of offenses but I wanted to distance myself from the vehicle as much as possible, thinking it had to at least be trespass. I tried to walk casually but purposefully as if I belonged in this neighbourhood. The front of my clothes were now dry but the back, where it was squashed against the leather was still damp and probably very wrinkled. As I passed rows of small houses with front gardens I noticed pots of herbs in nearly all of them. I backed up and cast my eyes over the pots. In the third front garden I found what I was after. The house was still dark so I stepped onto the front path and knelt in front of a very large pot with an abundance of green leaves. I rubbed one of the leaf tips between my fingers and then held my fingers to my nose. Small victory, it was mint. I'd have preferred spearmint but peppermint would have to do. I ripped off two leaves and stepped back to the pavement, continuing my exploration of the area while munching the leaves that would abrade my teeth and cleanse my morning breath. It was a much better start to this day than yesterday had been.

I had wandered for hours and now knew every inch of Barnes. At nine o'clock when the stores opened I wandered back to the High street.

As I rummaged in the charity shop, Barnes Cares, I thought to myself, I have become Raffles. A millionaire thief. Circumstances force me to steal again. The lie has become the truth. I was heartened, though, that my crimes were de-escalating. Speed boat, then designer frock and accoutrement. Now it would be cheap jeans and a top from this self-titled store in this altruistic posh neighbourhood.

I garnered the items from the rail and slid into the dressing room without the harried clerk noticing my dewy, wrinkled dress and sweater. Laura Ashley, Cath Kidston or whatever floral of the month I wore blended well in Barnes. I changed into the casual togs and hung the dress and cardigan on the empty hangars. With false bravado I walked out of the dressing room and hung them on the sales rack, then calmly left the shop. Some of my guilt was assuaged by knowing that again I left greater value than I took.

Dejection returned, as had become the aftermath of each narrow escape, and tears returned with the memory of Josh and his horrific death. I could kid myself that the River Boat officers were thrown clear of the explosion but it clearly came from the houseboat and it was impossible that anyone on board could survive. I let the tears fall as I wandered. I kept walking because I didn't know how else to make the minutes pass. The high street offered no familiar chains to window shop in or around anonymously. A small Italian cafe solicited a sous chef by a small notice in its front window. I pushed on the door thinking I could waste a few minutes entreating details of the post. A handsome man in chef whites rose from a table in the back dominated by chits and charts. I enquired after the job and the chef shook my hand. "Go cook me something," he said with a hint of an accent, "lunch, not breakfast." He went back to his receipts and I scanned the back interior for the entrance to the kitchen.

I was flabbergasted but also relieved. He had asked no questions so I had told no lies. Cooking was always honest and felt good. I assembled ingredients and began the beautiful alchemy of turning flour and oil into pasta. The manual labour eased the tension in my muscles and the repetitive movements eased my mind. I relaxed as I rolled and cut the silky sheets laying them out to accept the seasoned filling for a simple garlic spinach, ricotta and pine nut ravioli. Finishing the prep I laid the parcels gently into a pot of simmering water and set about coaxing a lemon sauce from a knob of butter, white wine, shaved rind of sunshine fruit, some chopped rosemary, and salt & pepper. I then plated two bowls with the translucent ravioli and glossed them with the sauce. Carrying the bowls through I was giddy that I would get to eat without having to steal. The chef checked his watch as I emerged and managed a half smile which turned to a raised eyebrow as I sat with my own food opposite him at the table. Wordlessly we ate, the silence not companionable but not objectionable. I was satisfied with the dish and grateful to be eating. When we had both consumed our meals entirely I lifted the bowls and set off back for the kitchen.

"When can you start?" the chef lilted after me. "After I make a phone call," I replied, surprising myself as I hadn't thought past washing the dishes. Clearly I couldn't accept the job, but it would be nice to have a haven for the day. It occurred to me that I had been running without my own purpose, happy to let Matt lead the way. I guessed his aim was to keep me close while trying to puzzle an acceptable solution. My mission was clearly exoneration, but I would be happy to put as much distance behind myself and London, figuring a solution from Hawaii if possible; it just didn't seem possible with no money, no clothes, in fact, no resources other than my muddled wit. I'd rectify that now and use the day to formulate a plan; and to figure out whose scope had targeted me in its sight.

I found a phone on the kitchen wall and dialled Matt's office again. It was answered by a machine relating that Matt was working from home today. I dialled his home number and he answered on the first ring. "It's bugged," Matt's sharp tone warned. "Just checking," I rushed out in a single breath. "King's Head, dark," Matt responded and rang off quickly. I hoped the BBC was right and it wasn't long enough for anyone to trace the call. I hoped that by now Matt had discerned that I meant the Kings Head in Fulham which was a regular haunt for musos. I hoped that the other three in West London were as well so that whoever was listening wouldn't know which one. A combined effort of all law enforcement agencies would be needed to stake out all the Kings Head pubs in London.

I headed back to the kitchen, relieved to have heard Matt's soothing voice again, even for a split second and to have an occupation for the next 12 hours. I remembered our last conversation. Saying the words out loud tore at my soul, "Josh is dead." I stopped myself from reeling at the loss of Josh again by studying the menu and deciding to prep onions first so my tears would be misconstrued.

Hours later I stood at the stove mesmerized by the flames; blue at the base and blazoning out into crimsons and ambers. I was mutely rooted to the spot unable to run though my mind bid my feet to move and my throat to scream. The flame surrounding the red pepper blistering in the heat triggered flashbacks of yesterday's explosion. Rather than cave to the emotion I let the scene rewind to the events preceding, "Explosion, river chase, Soho, rooftops, Bond, Harrods, car chase, Guildford, body in my house, arrest, after party, Zulu." I stopped at Zulu. Sensory memory sparked. Walker was there! He was one of the blue suits in the large conference room, waiting for the files Josh was loathe to relinquish. Walker was also my arresting officer, interrogator and pursuer. I now knew that the answer lay in the files but that the files were at Josh's and were destroyed by the explosion. Even if I couldn't prove it, I knew the answer had to be in the overpayments. The overpayments were royalties to Johnny; the interrogation centred on my account from Johnny's royalties; Johnny was at the after party and was due at my house. I staggered from fear as I thought the dead body being removed from my house was Johnny and that he'd been killed. I'd lost both men in my life in a single day. I pulled the pepper off the stove and sealed it in brown paper to steam so the blistered skin would peel easily. I grabbed the phone and dialled Johnny's number. The organized chaos around me from the other kitchen workers went uninterrupted. While not hostile to the new employee, they hadn't embraced me either and just left me to my own chores and morose, troubled demeanour. The phone rang and I waited through 20 peals punctuated by ominous silence. Although I knew the veracity of the situation, I couldn't handle the conscious thought of Johnny being dead too, murdered. I passed a bottle of Pernod on my way back to the stove and thought back to tequila and something Johnny had said at the after party, How would I check for money laundering? I still didn't know but I was sure it was the key to this nightmare.

I floated through service in a daze and approached Marco, as I now knew his name. "I'm sorry chef, this isn't for me," I apologized. "Not today," he consoled, "but come back when your soul is no longer troubled." He handed me £40 and hugged me, an uncharacteristic move for a chef. Grateful, I returned the embrace, internally vowing to return but just to recount the tale and cement the new friendship over several drinks; and to garner some recipes for a new cookbook.

I had just enough time to hop a cab and fly over Putney Bridge into Fulham to the New Kings Road. At 8pm it was too early for the headline band to play and, as I hoped, there was a large crowd milling about outside. I scanned the crowd for Matt, my mind's eye a shutter lens, regretting that I didn't have my camera to capture the anticipatory faces of the crowd. Livingston was making a rare small venue UK appearance, rare because they now headlined arenas in Europe and the States. I'd really loved to have seen them, Beukes Willemse being an old dear friend, but I would never have let my misfortune and the ensuing danger touch him.

Scrutinizing faces in the crowd outside, I espied a beat patrolman approaching the pack. I dropped to a crouch attracting attention rather than evading it. The immediate crowd looked at me, and then looked around, noticing the uniformed cop. Rockers were notoriously rebellious and excitement swelled among them. A squeal of tires tore through the murmurs and I stood up to see the red Boxster peel to a stop, Matt at the wheel having seen me before the Bobby did. I tried to run but the crowd had other ideas and lifted me then laid me prone handing me from person to person mosh pit style. The very aware Met cop finally recognized me and tried to intervene, but could gain no purchase being kept outside the dense throng. I was handed to the passenger side of the Porsche and then another set of arms grabbed me around the waist as the car sped off with me impersonating a wing mirror, the policeman already on his radio calling in the sighting.

The car raced back towards the Putney Bridge and careened around a corner. The arms relaxed and I fell to the pavement. The passenger door swung open and the arms grabbed me again, pulling me onto the passenger seat. I screamed. I thought I was being manhandled by a ghost. Josh was dead, but he was there in the car.

"Lola! Stop! I'm here," Josh screamed as I beat at his face, expecting my fists to fly through his form.

"You're dead! I saw your boat explode," I wailed.

"Lola he's not dead. He wasn't home. He was with me. He's not dead," Matt tried to explain.

"My house is gone?" Josh worried.

We were all shouting at once but their words penetrated my hysteria. I twisted in my seat for a better view of the man both cushioning me and pressing me into the dashboard. He looked real and felt real. I desperately wanted to believe he was alive and one whiff of his Angel for Men legitimated the belief. Relieved, I hugged him as best I could and beamed at Matt.

"It's the files," I blurted, excited, "money laundering, Johnny's account. Mine too. Is Johnny alive too?" For a moment I was hopeful, but in the pause that followed I knew he wasn't, the silence quashing the hope.

"I'm sorry babe," Matt offered, "we know about the accounting and we're off to find the rest of your files as proof. We'll be tracked but we're ahead for now and they can't anticipate our destination."

Matt drove us south along the A23 to Brighton after turning off the South Circular Road. Normally he would have headed to the M25 to avoid the hordes of traffic, but at this late hour the road was eighty percent deserted. Matt was not used to having to think about the 30mph speed limit on the suburban streets because he usually kept to a snail's pace, bumper to bumper with all the other city drivers. He drove cautiously tonight keeping his eye on the prize and not wanting to be pulled over by any kind of law enforcement official not only because I was a person of interest, but also because he had one too many passengers in the front seat.

Josh and I were seated awkwardly, me between Josh's spread-eagled legs. It made it even more uncomfortable each time I turned around to check that Josh was really there. Finally I said, "I'm glad you're not dead."

Josh smiled but asked, "Is my house really gone?"

"Is that all you can think about?" I said shocked, "I was devastated."

"That I'm not dead?" I had often wondered if Josh had an inability to read me or any other person's facial expression or tone of voice and might have Asperger's Syndrome or whether his sense of humour was just inappropriate and tactless. I let the thought go for now.

We followed the A road until it became the M23 and then again when the motorway ended. After about an hour and ten minutes we turned left onto Lewes Road then weaved our way through side streets to Coombe Road and the ten foot high gates surrounding the cavernous white building and deserted parking lot. Finally the car pulled up to the outer gates of the Big Yellow Box storage facilities on the huge industrial estate. It was pitch dark, but for the eerie glow in the inner depths of the glass fronted office. Josh gave Matt the security code and Matt leaned out of the window. When he touched the first button on the security keypad, it lit up and glowed green, a security light by the internal grate simultaneously lighting. Matt typed in the rest of the code, prompted by Josh although Matt hadn't forgotten it in the previous second. The gate slid silently open. We drove in and parked as near the front grate as possible. The three of us struggled out of the car and walked noiselessly to the internal grate, its keypad already illuminated. Josh entered that code and the grate ascended.

Upon entering, we crossed a knee high beam which triggered the grate's descent behind us. Motion sensor lights lit our path as we walked. The interior was a maze of white corridors flanked by yellow metal grates. The metal grates hid storage units of various sizes. The ceilings of the units were artificially lower than the ceiling of the building itself with CCTV cameras at every intersection. The layout was basically a 16 box tic tac toe grid if viewed from above. Josh led us through the grid to his, our unit.

I knew that Josh had stored the detritus of our marriage at his parents but should have estimated that it wasn't really a possibility in their downsized bungalow; I also knew he had this storage unit but I thought he had given me a key merely to engender sympathy for the cramped quarters of the houseboat. I felt a moment of shame that I hadn't cared enough to ponder it more at the time. I was just relieved not to be responsible for an over-aged boy still trying to live the rock and roll dream. Peering at Josh through heavy lids now, it further saddened me to think that he was only able to grow up in my absence and that my presence stunted his development. No girl wanted to admit that she was the problem rather than the salvation. I was maudlin in the irrational epiphany that my death would have benefited Josh whereas belief in his demise brought my devastation. While not a catharsis, that knowledge brought me an unhealthy peace. I didn't have to run or fight; my existence was irrelevant. All my fear vanished and I was at the depths again of my emotional roller coaster.

Josh pulled out a key chain and located a small key that opened the large Yale lock. He removed the lock, lifted the gate slightly and replaced the lock in its hole so it didn't get lost amongst whatever they found. He manually lifted the noisy gate. After all the quiet grates, its noise was surprisingly loud. The anterior store room was alarmingly crowded, teeming with boxes and flight cases. The rear was lined with neatly stacked and labelled boxes. The front however looked haphazard, the accumulation of an entire life chaotically abandoned. I recognized it as the contents of Johnny's house; cleared for the renovation that put him in harm's way at my flat. With a gut-wrenching pain, I accepted his death yet again. It hurt just as much as before but I welcomed the pain now in the comforting knowledge that I would likely join him soon.

We pulled out Johnny's belongings and unloaded them in the corridor, Matt and Josh erecting a fortress as boys always do without forethought. My eyes alit on a case of tequila, Johnny's trademark Cuervo Gold. A jolt stabbed at my heart yet again.

"How did Johnny die?" I asked. I had assumed he was shot because so many people were shooting at me but I had no actual knowledge.

"His tequila was poisoned with bleach. They found the poisoned remains of a worm in his throat," Matt explained gently, "and they're ruling it a suicide because they found a note. It said that he couldn't face the discovery of the tax cheat and money laundering."

That rankled my new desolate tranquillity. Like a bad photo, it was out of focus with a tree blocking the serene view. I opened the case of booze to confirm what I already knew: tequila, especially Jose's oro nectar, didn't have worms, only mezcal did.

Then Matt added the final stone to shatter my new found serenity, "It also named you as a willing accomplice."

My serenity shattered again, I was irate, "Then why the hell are we here? Whoever killed him has framed me convincingly."

"We need your bank statements," Matt answered. He knew I would not take the news well but he didn't want a confrontation just yet.

"Why? They already have them!" I yelled.

"Because these are unopened," Matt replied neutrally.

"So?"

"They evidence that you didn't access the account."

"They're no better evidence than the opened ones."

"They are. They imply that you didn't know how much money you had because you didn't know about the laundering."

I was growing angrier, this time at Matt. "No they don't. I could still have known and not opened them because I already knew and didn't need verification. I didn't, but it doesn't prove anything."

Matt whirled on me, "Look! If you knew and you were a part of the plan you would likely have been paid through an account you controlled. The absence of withdrawal slips, internet codes and phone calls to the bank, together with the unopened statements corroborate your testimony that you didn't. We don't have to prove anything. These will make it harder for them to prove knowledge, suspicion or cooperation. It's the best we can do."

"Then I'm still in big trouble."

"You're welcome."

"Do they still think I killed Johnny? Now that they have a note?"

"I don't know."

"If they find the note credible in framing me for the money crime, then they have to find it credible in exonerating me from the murder." I didn't really find comfort there, I was merely thinking out loud. Then I shouted, "Those fucking wankers!" I was bouncing from the depths of despair to the brink of anarchy; my disposition kept changing in an instant. Josh knew this mood and slid further into the unit. "That's their second mistake!" I bellowed just as Josh re-emerged with a box of files. "Tequila doesn't have worms and Johnny only drinks tequila. He'd never have taken it willingly. He was murdered and the note was a fake."

"We figured that but we need these additional files to trace the money over the entire period." explained Matt.

The eerie glow of the top left monitor in the storage facility's office flickered as a dark figure moved past the camera's lens. The figure passed from the first screen to the next with a steady pace and cautious posture. Facial features were indiscernible but the height and flat chest girth indicated a man. He was slightly hunched as if ready to pounce or plant his feet and take aim. In his hand was a large gun, its precise calibre not evident to an untrained eye. The cameras followed him through four screens. Then he was gone. Had the monitors been manned, the operator could have adjusted the angle and followed him as he climbed atop a unit grid.

It occurred to the gunman that he was now playing tic tac toe as the grid implied. He felt like the master manipulator as he watched the heads of Lola, Matt and Josh, move in and out of range. He drowned out their voices which detracted from his omnipotence, imagining them only to have the thoughts he would give them.

"How did he die exactly? What does bleach do?" Josh asked.

"And why didn't it disintegrate the worm?"

"I don't know," said Matt slowly, a thought forming. He stopped pawing at boxes and stood up, pulling out his wallet. He extracted Cecil's card from the soft leather. "Josh, do you have a phone?"

Josh handed his phone to Matt who punched the number into Josh's mobile. "I'm calling Detective Cecil to let him know we're coming in."

"Are you insane?" I shrieked querulously, "I'm not going back to jail."

"Lola there's already a police warrant for your arrest," retorted Matt. "You stand a better chance of appearing voluntarily and presenting the exonerating evidence first." Matt dialled and waited. Josh and I just stared at him, wondering what he was up to.

Cecil finally answered distractedly and grumbled on the other end of the line, "Do you know what time it is?"

Matt's reply was abrupt, "No. Matt Stephens Gilbert here. What exactly was the cause of death?"

"Where are you? Where's Lola Steele?" Cecil was fully engaged now.

"How did Johnny Hathaway die?"

"Damn it this is serious. Lola was abducted by two men in a red Porsche with dealer plates. We're trying to locate the dealership manager to see if it was stolen."

"It wasn't. She's with me."

"You drive a BMW."

"For fuck's sake it's a loaner. Cause of death?!?" Matt heard Cecil slap some hard surface in frustration for not having guessed or at least speculated more intelligently.

"Poisoned worm in his tequila. Her alibi is no good, the bleach could have been added before her arrest. You have to bring her in."

"Ok, I will. We'll be back in London tomorrow." Matt held his hand over the mouthpiece and turned to us, "He just says poisoned worm in his tequila."

The gunman watched as his game pieces stood still; he allowed the voices to drift back and realized with fright that Matt was on the phone. That was not a move he could allow. He flattened his crouched form prone and took aim. With a sharp intake of breath he squeezed the trigger and watched as

Matt dropped the mobile handset as the bullet whizzed closely by his expensively cropped hair and hit a box on the floor. Tinkling pealed and hail blew skyward as glass bottles shattered and flew. It was a magical moment spoiled only by the absence of blood and brain.

The explosion of the fire pin and the echo of the chamber as the bullet exited the gun were easily identifiable by Cecil. He also heard the shattering of glass and it confused his identification of ambient sounds. He was unable to identify their location by audible clues.

In the storage warehouse, we were startled by the cacophony and momentarily frozen, then we each reacted as if our on switch had been flipped, diving in opposite directions.

"Jesus! Where are you?" Cecil shouted into the phone which Matt had dropped as he dashed around the right-hand corner. Josh flung himself to the left hand corner and pulled his legs around, pressing himself against the unit wall. I fell into the unit landing on my side; peripherally I could see the phone lying just outside the open gate; I crawled forward and reached out my hand, grabbed the phone and stumbled back into the unit, scrambling to its rear, hoping for safety before realizing I was trapping myself.

"Hello? What was that?" scratched Cecil's tinny voice from the phone in my hand.

"They're shooting at me again! Who keeps shooting at me?" I was hysterical again.

"Miss Steele? Is that you? Where are you?" replied Cecil excitedly.

The gunman had seen the three separate and hesitated wondering which to follow. They were out of his line of sight in his prone position. He tried to stand but was too tall so he crouched again and manoeuvred himself to the edge. He could see Josh as he traversed the corridors, checking all doors for unlocked store cupboards. The gunman smiled inwardly at the thought of a broom or dustpan in a shootout with his weapon. Deciding Josh posed no threat, he searched for Matt without success.

I cried into the phone, "I didn't kill Johnny! I didn't steal any money!" My screaming was like an arrow divulging my location within the confines of the unit.

"I know honey," soothed Cecil. "We know who did and we just have some questions for you. Where are you? I'll come and save you. Tell me where you are," coaxed Cecil.

"Save me?!? What year do you live in? Do you job properly and save yourself. I'm still lawyer you know!" I knew I wasn't making sense but I was angry at the manipulation and misogyny. I stopped talking to consider which made me more angry.

The gunman couldn't see her but he heard her and followed the sound of her agitated voice. He couldn't get a clear angle into the unit as he was parallel to it so he stood as best he could, backed up to the rear edge of his cube and ran. He leapt across the gap between the unit cubes, like OJ Simpson in the Hertz adverts, the irony of murder not being lost on him. He landed atop the unit across from Lola. He could now easily see inside from this angle; he felt like a Greek god surveying the mortals from Mount Olympus. Then his thoughts abruptly shifted and he felt like he was at a fun fair. He aimed his pistol at the duck and pulled the trigger waiting expectantly for it to bend backwards with a clang.

I heard and felt the shot simultaneously with my right ear, a cool breeze traversing the top and a horrible pulse jamming into the canal. I screamed.

There was another bang which impacted the right side of my waist, spun me around and knocked me on my face. I felt my side to see if the spot was sore and would bruise. It was numb, but wet and sticky.

"I'm in the boxes. I'm bleeding," I whispered breathless rather than cautious.

"No, where are you geographically?" Cecil asked, his patience evaporating.

"GPS," I thought, might have even said aloud. My head was lolling and my eyes caught sight of a box marked kitchen. I dropped the phone and used both hands to grapple it open. The kitchen had been my haven always, even in the last few nightmare days. I sought some level of comfort from the remnants of a kitchen that once felt like home.

Both Matt and Josh heard the additional shots and raced back to the unit returning at the same time. The gunman waited until they were close together then pounced from his aerie perch, landing on both of them and sending them flying. He grabbed at Josh's back to inhibit further flight and chopped him on the head with the butt of the pistol. Josh fell to the floor slowly like a collapsing house of cards. Matt recovered from his spill, found his feet and lunged for the murderous intruder.

I heard the crash and a series of grunts outside the unit and sensed rather than witnessed the brawl in front of me somewhere, the sound and the heat of the explosions rocking back my memories of the houseboat explosion and causing flashbacks of grief and turmoil. The shooter was after Matt and Josh! I thought that I had lost Josh once and was not about to lose him again; nor was I going to let Matt die especially after losing Johnny to this monster. Fury spiked again and I plunged into the box marked kitchen with purpose.

I pulled out various bottles and boxes normally housed under the sink and in the fridge, combining liquids and powders in a Tupperware container like a mad scientist. It had non-dairy creamer, hand sanitizer and potpourri. I groped in the box again and pulled out a candle, ripping out its wick and placing it in the container with its end dangling outside the lid as I sealed it shut around three edges. One final forage and I found a box of matches.

I needed to draw the attention of the murderous hulk away from my men. I could see him scrapping with Matt, and Josh lying on the floor nearby. I grabbed the first bulky item I could find and flung it at the big bastard. The large golden replica statue of The Daughter of Xerxes shattered as it hit him on the shoulder. He spun around but was unfazed by the impact. It was Walker! He was blinded by the white powder storming about his head and stumbling. I struck a match to the wick, the container lying on the floor still at the rear of the unit.

"Run! Get back!" I screamed at Matt, racing for the front of the unit. I flew out and shoved Walker into the unit, pulling down the gate and locking him inside. I heard him tumble to the floor and land with a thud. I grabbed Josh by the collar and heaved him around the corner, Matt at my heels, just as an explosion erupted from the locked unit. The gate buckled but held, spewing white powder through the tiny gaps.

As the dust settled, thunder rumbled and the floor shuddered beneath us but it wasn't coming from the storage unit. The commotion stopped as suddenly as it started. "Police! Step out slowly with your hands up." It was a command, not a request.

Matt poked his head around the corner and advanced slowly, one hand raised and the other dragging Josh, who was finally starting to come around, to my great relief. I must have been holding my breath because I let out a momentous sigh, but as I let the air escape, I also seemed to be letting the lights dim and sending the voices into a vast aluminium can. I last saw blurry uniformed figures approaching as I fell further away into the peace and calm of oblivion.

Just after midnight

Cecil drove through the gates as Matt and Josh were being led out by several uniformed officers in riot gear. An EMT escorted by another uniformed officer, rolled out a gurney with me swathed in sheets and strapped down, looking more like a psychiatric patient than a shooting victim. As the EMT lifted the gurney into the ambulance, Cecil walked over to Matt and removed his handcuffs. Then he motioned for an officer to do the same with Josh. Cecil eyed Matt and said, "I assume you'll come voluntarily. To my office. Not to the cells."

"Of course. Assuming you'll come to the hospital first."

"Of course," Cecil replied without hesitation then turned to the EMT, "How bad is she?"

The EMT, an athletic woman in her thirties, disliked any delay in the performance of her care. She would never get used to the indifference of non-medical professionals to the precious seconds that were wasted with this kind of chat so she answered tersely, "She's stable," then added, "for now," to disquiet any further conversation. She then raced back to the cab of the vehicle to emphasize the point that they were in a rush to save lives. As her door latched closed, her partner drove the ambulance away and the matter was closed, fully and finally.

Two gentlemen from the coroner's office exited the building next, a body bag on another gurney between them. Cecil stopped them as they pulled close, on way to their own van then turned to a SOCO technician laden with several clear evidence bags containing the gun, artefacts, powder, tequila bottle fragments and Tupperware fragments. Cecil pointed to the bag with the white powder and asked, "Positive?" The scientist answered in the affirmative and continued to his utility vehicle.

Cecil turned back to the medical examiner with a questioning look. The doctor nodded and Cecil unzipped the bag just enough to see the face of the deceased. The head, still partially masked in black wool, was gory from the explosion. Matt came up behind Cecil and waited, peering at the gunman. Cecil peeled away the charred pieces of mask revealing DI Stuart Walker.

Cecil sighed, "Not the way I wanted to get him."

Matt was querulous, "You knew?"

"I suspected. I was gathering evidence."

"What were you hoping for?"

"An example. A long custodial sentence for him and the others. To rid this system of an endemically corrupt agency operating outside the law, thinking it's above the law."

Matt studied Cecil's face searching for a hint of sarcasm, "Really?"

Cecil smiled sardonically and said, "No. Just hoping for a medal and a promotion."

Matt smiled, slightly relieved.

Cecil signalled to another officer and called him over for instructions, "These two," he said pointing at Matt and Josh, "will ride with me to the hospital. You take their car," pointing to the Porsche, "to the lab, it's evidence now." Matt winced fathoming the amount of legal hounding and paperwork it would take to get his own car back from the dealer but he tossed the keys to the copper anyway, knowing he had no choice.

The uniformed Bobby hesitated waiting for someone to tell him it was just a joke. When no one did he grinned widely praising the universe for his good luck; he was going to drive a Porsche! Cecil snapped, "Hey. Let's not forget someone was shot here today so you could get this joy ride." The young officer's face fell ashamedly and he slinked away to the bright red car.

"That was a little harsh," said Matt.

"Actually, I was just making sure he took it straight to the lab. At his age I'd have driven around for a bit, possibly shown it off to my friends."

I lay in the hard bed thinking that it was nice to be sleeping without dreaming; no nightmares finally. I could do with a softer mattress but for now perhaps just a different position would do. When I tried to adjust myself, a searing pain tore into my side as I fought for movement. I opened my eyes to harsh silver lighting bouncing off pristine white tiles. I turned my head from side to side and saw chrome railings and small unidentifiable monitors trailing tubes towards pulleys and to my bed. Coherence dawned: I was in a hospital bed and trussed around my torso. The wince that escaped from my pained face brought the attention of those around me. I recognized Matt and a bandaged Josh immediately but took longer to identify Cecil as the officer outside my house a number of days previously. I'd lost track of time and couldn't grasp which event belonged to which day.

"I didn't do it. Any of it," I cried as I struggled to get up so I could escape and run again. The cries of innocence melded into sobs of pain as I thrashed about. Restraining hands tried to settle me but were less effective than the agony of the gunshot wound torturing me into submission.

"I know you didn't," soothed Cecil, "you're not under arrest."

"He knew about Walker," said Matt, "the officer who arrested you."

"Then why didn't you arrest him instead of coming after me?" I was still losing tears but was no longer sobbing.

"I needed your evidence," Cecil replied.

"Why?" I asked. "You could have at least arrested him to stop him trying to kill me!"

"I needed an example not a corpse," replied Cecil.

I was so confused. "But Zulu are the thieves. They were stealing and laundering the money. The files prove that they were complicit."

"They were certainly the architects, but they couldn't have moved that much money just on royalties," Cecil explained. "In countries with currency restrictions they were buying merchandise, shipping it out of that country and selling it in countries from which they could send the money back to the UK."

"That's not illegal. Bands have been doing it since the 70s," I argued.

"True," countered Cecil, "but after a while it wasn't enough for them. They began smuggling priceless artefacts in with the replicas. There was no need to bring the merchandise into the UK if the money was already here. So the merchandise had to have value itself, but outwardly, it didn't. And smuggling on that large a scale could only get past ESCU if they weren't looking."

"Who killed Johnny and tried to kill Josh?" I asked, still worried.

"That's a good question Ms Steele," said Cecil in a tone dripping with allegation. "Your prints were on the bottle of tequila found in your house, you were present at the destruction of Mr Steele's houseboat where three police officers were injured and their cruiser destroyed and another body was found; you have just blown up and killed an agent of her Majesty's government and last but not least there's a priceless antique in your storage unit. You may not have been a part of the financial crimes but you still have a lot to answer for."

"Don't say a word Lola," instructed Matt assuming his role of protector.

"Relax counsellor," advised Cecil wearily, "I'm not serious. She's not under arrest but she could offer to help me with my inquiries. Things go very wrong when I try to arrest her"

"We all will," chimed Josh, "if you get us out of here now. That sink bomb still smells disgusting on my clothes." Josh's head was bandaged and he looked green around the gills but he seemed otherwise well. Only Matt escaped a gauze makeover.

"Agreed," Matt, Cecil and I concurred simultaneously.

Cecil looked at me the way he would an errant child. "You're staying here overnight, for observation."

I started to protest.

"If you argue with me I'll have you handcuffed to the bed," he barked, then added in a softer tone, "You can't testify if you rip open your wound and bleed out. Just promise that you'll come straight to my office when they release you tomorrow."

To Matt he added, "You're an officer of the court, I'm ordering you to stay with her; she's never to be out of your sight and she's your responsibility." Then he turned to Josh and said, "I'm also deputising you to do the same, as he was so useless at bringing her in last time."

"Can he do that?" Josh asked Matt.

"No," replied Matt matter of factly, "This isn't America."

Cecil chuckled and said, "Then I'll just shoot whoever fails at this task."

The next day

Matt, Josh and I were seated in front of Cecil's desk in chairs gathered hickledy pickledy from other desks. Apparently, Cecil didn't usually have this many visitors at one time. I had a bandaged arm in a sling and my stiff erect posture indicated that I was still bound around the waist and in pain. My hair was unkempt and still mottled with river filth and my clothes were bloodstained and wrinkled. The only part of me that was clean was my face, which had been scrubbed and showed signs of dermabrasion.

Cecil began the informal interview without the formalities or the aid of a tape recorder, "Your fingerprints were on both bottles Ms. Steele."

"It was my house Detective Cecil. The mezcal and the tequila were purchased by me. The important thing is tequila doesn't have worms. Only mezcal does. Johnny didn't drink mezcal. He only ever had one shot of Cuervo Gold per day. Nothing else. Ever. He was a recovering alcoholic."

"Maybe you knew he'd fall off the wagon one day and you were just waiting."

"Then I'd have bought him Jack Daniels. He loved JD but hated tequila. That's how he was able to keep to one shot per day. Like medicine. With JD he drank until the bottle was empty. I wouldn't have needed to poison him. He'd have been dead in a year from liver failure."

"And you Mr. Steele? A man died in your house too. How do you explain that?"

"Really? I can't. I didn't know. Who? I wasn't expecting anyone? Hey, I wouldn't blow up my own home." Josh was genuinely surprised having missed the reference to this other corpse at the hospital yesterday.

"Your wife blew up the contents of two homes, and as I understand, the evidence that exonerates her in the fraud case." Cecil raised an eyebrow at them.

Matt intervened sensing accusation, an occupational hazard, "We can still rely on live witnesses. Her defence is still good."

Cecil wrinkled his face, "Thank you counsellor. My point is that people do stupid things. Mr. Steele your victim was dead before the explosion. Gunshot wound, small calibre, close range."

"Who was it?" Josh asked again.

"Didn't I say? One Jake Drake – stupid name – Johnny Hathaway's solicitor. So I have a dead rock star, his dead lawyer and his accountant and ex-girlfriend, your ex-wife, in my office. I don't believe in coincidences."

Again Matt interrupted, "I don't think it is a coincidence. I think it started with Lola's arrest. They were using her account to launder the proceeds of fraud."

"Unfortunately the fraud was a compounded felony. They were also smuggling goods, which doesn't really fit the pattern," countered Cecil, "Each shipment of reproduction artefacts had one real piece which should never have left its country of origin," Cecil added into the mix.

"So the chain had to include: the record company to buy the goods, Someone to clear it in the UK without questions, and buyers in the UK to pay for it. Drug dealers are easy but who could afford the art?" wondered Matt following the thread.

"I've got that nailed but I still have to find Drake's killer."

"McDonald," I piped in.

"Who?" asked Cecil.

"Rupert McDonald," added Josh, "The record company connection. I have the documents to prove his collusion. He let me have them by mistake when Jake interrupted our meeting. That's probably why they blew up my house. The papers and I should have been home by then. If I hadn't been camping out on Matt's door step..." Josh shuddered at the thought then continued, "A dozen neighbours and one impatient barista will vouch for my whereabouts."

Cecil shook his head, feeling worried that his case was about to fall apart, "Record companies don't kill people. They make millions and don't have to."

"You are so naive. Sony was the biggest beneficiary of Michael Jackson's death," I pointed out.

"You're telling me that Sony killed Michael Jackson?!?!" said Cecil querulously.

"No, but Jacko was $600million unrecouped and they knew they were never going to see that money in his lifetime. They had enough life insurance on him for the majority of it."

"It's illegal if Jackson didn't know" stated Cecil.

"He did. All artists agree to a medical for just that purpose when they sign their recording agreements."

"You haven't convinced me that record companies commit crimes against their artists," Cecil said, feeling a little unsettled.

"Again, Michael Jackson. A rival major label orchestrated the first child molestation allegations hoping that Sony would drop him and they could pick him up cheaply. Well cheap for Michael Jackson."

"But he was accused again and there was enough evidence to take him to trial," argued Cecil, "there's no smoke without fire."

"Rubbish," I snapped, "he was an easy target after the first time; mud sticks and people will take advantage." I was feeling a bit of fire now, not because I felt MJ's memory needed protecting but because Cecil was close minded to the theory of multi nationals being run by unscrupulous individuals.

"Lola, he had boys sleep in his bedroom, that's just twisted," patronized Cecil.

"You idiot!" I exploded, "His bedroom not his bed. And the room was 1000 square feet! Bigger than most Manhattan apartments. And the evidence was the testimony of the accusers who were found not credible. Why am I arguing justice with you? You should believe in the system."

"I've seen too many undeserved acquittals," replied Cecil, tiring.

"And I've seen too many record company executives doing immoral things believing themselves underpaid or undervalued. In my experience, the more an industry is perceived to be glamorous and exciting, the more vile the people it attracts. But to be fair, McDonald wasn't smart enough to orchestrate this complexity. I'd also look at the CFO and the CEO."

Cecil didn't want to argue anymore. He just wanted all the information necessary to wrap up this investigation. He certainly didn't want to make an enemy of me.

Matt enjoyed his ring side seat at this banter, but now that it was winding down he worried at the thread again, "Who did they sell to?"

Brought back to the real issues, Cecil answered Matt directly, "The art went to London society – a select circle. Walker was quite a high flyer for a lowly civil servant. In fact I'm also looking at Parliament. At every face on his wall of fame. What kind of cop gets photgrahed with rock stars and politicians?"

"I still don't understand why Walker arrested Lola in the first place if it would open a can of worms for him," mused Matt.

"To control the investigation," explained Cecil. "She was part of a larger operation that was about to unwind and the arrest was ordered by someone higher. He had to take charge before any fingers were pointed at him; what better way than to point the finger at her. He knew she didn't know and couldn't point it back."

"That's evil," I said.

"All crime is, to the victim," said Cecil in a welcome to my world tone of voice.

Having all the missing pieces, Cecil was once again in a position to request search and arrest warrants. This time, however, he would approach the one Judge he knew wasn't corrupt, Judge Marilyn Leventhal. She had dismissed or overturned hundreds of ESCU cases in the past few years, several cases instituted by Matt's firm.

Cecil entered the hallowed halls of the Southwark Crown Court where Judge Leventhal was presiding over a murder trial. The irony of the court's placement near the London Dungeons was never lost on Cecil. He had timed his arrival to coincide with the end of the lunch intermission so as not to interrupt her meal, such was his respect for the Judge.

As he approached her chambers, the clerk sitting at the desk outside smiled and said, "We've been expecting you."

"Good news travels fast. Almost as fast as bad news," Cecil smiled back. She rose and opened the door to the inner chamber.

Marilyn Leventhal was the exception to the rule. She was comfortable and completely at ease within her body and soul. Her preference was for simple linen and cotton suits classically constructed without being too Kings Road or Sloane Ranger. Her naturally greyed hair was cut simply framing her friendly face nicely. Cecil knew that the friendliness could turn to sternness if anyone tried to play the fool in her courtroom and the chill that emanated from her ice blue eyes could make an East End gangster wet his pants. Today, however, she was all smiles, thrilled to be a part of the huge changes about to be wrought.

"Detective," she beamed, "how are you?"

"Very well M'Lady," Cecil returned, "and you?"

"Smashing. Simply smashing. Now what have you brought for me?"

Cecil handed over the fat file he held tightly; he had been crushing it in his fingers for the past 15 minutes, his journey time from New Scotland Yard to this place south of the river, for fear that the pages would disappear or fly away and the knowledge and evidence evaporating with it. He was greatly relieved to hand over the files and the responsibility for their care, if even for just the time it took for Judge Leventhal to sign the papers inside and hand them back.

The judge squared the papers just left of centre on the desk and set about signing each one after a peremptory scan on its contents. Only once or twice did she pause briefly and chuckle at the name on the page. At the penultimate one however, she sat back. "I didn't think you'd get this far," she said looking up at Cecil.

Cecil glanced over the desk and read the upside down name on the arrest warrant. It read, The Honourable Alice Walters, MP. "I hope you won't feel compromised," said

Cecil, giving Leventhal a chance to shy away from ordering the demise of a Member of Parliament.

Leventhal laughed out loud. “Au contraire,” she chortled, “I’ve been waiting for that bitch to screw up for years. We all knew she was up to something but we never knew what. I’m throwing a dinner party just to dine out on this story. Without giving away any privileged information or compromising the investigation of course.”

“Of course,” smiled Cecil broadly. “I’ll gladly send a bottle of fine champagne over for you and your guests to toast the occasion.”

With that Judge Leventhal signed the last two warrants, placed them neatly back in the folder and handed it back to Cecil.

“Thank you and good luck,” said Leventhal rising to shake Cecil’s hand.

“Not at all; thank you M’Lady,” said Cecil taking her hand and bowing courteously.

Detective Cecil, followed by four uniformed officers, pushed open the heavy oak doors from New Palace Yard in Westminster Palace to enter the House of Commons. Their heavy shoes thudded down the hallowed corridors to the Members offices. Heads peered from doorways. As they entered Minister Walters office their thundering stride drew her angry attention.

“This is not a public house!” she snapped, even though she knew her statement to be irrelevant and not caring.

Cecil was calm, not the least bit intimidated, although he was secretly excited. “Minister Alice Walters, I have a warrant for your arrest. You do not have to say anything, but it may harm your defence if you do not mention when questioned something which you may later rely on in court. Anything you do say may be given in evidence." The uniformed officers marched in pairs up to her desk.

Walters blinked furiously glaring first at Cecil, then at the men beside her one of whom had a pair of handcuffs at the ready.

"Do you know who I am?!?!" she sputtered, spitting in Cecil's direction, her spittle only reaching the papers on her desk. Her Private Secretary entered and glared at her superior of the past five years. She spun around and faced Cecil, squared her shoulders and informed him, "If you need any assistance in your enquiries, please let me know." She spun on her heel and strode towards the door. Walters picked up a heavy legal tome and threw it at the Secretary's back.

"Not only do I know who you are," replied Cecil with dignity, "I know what you are." To himself Cecil thought you are an arrogant holier than thou criminal who hates people and believes you are so far above the law that you can only look down upon it from your cloud, but aloud he merely said, "You are under arrest."

The officer with the handcuffs grabbed the Minister by the upper arm and tried to lift her up but was prevented by the slippery silk of her Armani suit. He nodded to the other officers and one of them stepped up to the Minister's other side. In unison they hooked her armpits in the crooks of their arms and lifted. Slowly the Minister began to rise, much to her surprise. She lifted her arms in the manner a baby does to wriggle out of its mother's hold, and fell back to her seat. The remaining two officers stepped in closer as titters erupted from the onlookers in the corridor. In an attempt to regain some of her lost dignity, Walters stood.

The policemen handcuffed the now erect Minister and led her unwillingly away towards the public exit.

"The Members exit!" she shouted. "If you please!"

Simultaneous to her undignified arrest, a SOCO team had entered Walters' home. The Caribbean maid sat nervously in a Louis XIV chair as they confiscated antiques, art and artefacts, testing surfaces for fingerprints and trace elements of who knew what.

Similarly, at the offices of Zulu Records, Cecil's colleague and two uniformed officers were arresting Rupert McDonald in his office, a SOCO team ready to roll in as they vacated the premises. While other record company executives and support staff watched intently, Lettie gawped with a mixture of fear and glee. Her fear for her continued employment and curiosity at what crime he could have committed was overshadowed by her joy at McDonald having his comeuppance in such a public and well viewed manner; even if it led to unemployment, she wouldn't have missed it for the world.

3 days later

Matt was sitting in my kitchen as I sealed the last platter of Manhattan prawn cocktail with cling film. I was still missing a load of stuff that had been confiscated by ESCU days before, but I managed to alter the menu for tonight's after-hours party for the Red Hot Chili Peppers. The theme was hot without actually using the word chilli in the names of the dishes. The cocktail sauce for this evening consisted of horseradish sauce and ketchup. Normally I would have grated and pounded the horseradish myself from scratch but being on the lam left me little time for preparation. The rest of the buffet would include crudités with Atomic Avocado Sauce which I found at horseradish.org, bruschetta with garlic tomatoes and basil, hot Singapore noodles, cold Chinese sesame noodles, Cajun popcorn, devilled eggs…you get the idea.

I had previously catered one of their tours and found it boring; they survived on mostly on fresh fruit and Starbucks Frappuccinos with the odd cold cut tray and vanilla soya milk chaser. I preferred the after-party gig as it came with room for creativity and actual cooking.

Matt was reading the daily paper and for the most part keeping out of my way. He began to read aloud, "It is believed the operation, the largest crime syndicate in UK history, began to unravel with the murder of rock legend, Johnny Hathaway and the false arrest of Lola Steele for whom Hathaway wrote Carry You Home which is being re-released by Zulu records. A spokesperson for Zulu said We are not cashing in on Johnny's death or McDonald's arrest; we are honouring his memory. The Metropolitan Police acknowledge the invaluable contribution of Ms Steele in bringing this gang to justice.' He must have a crush on you. You were just Watson to my Holmes. Where's my thanks?"

I had to laugh at that one, "Watson my ass. I'm Holmes. And Macgyver."

"Irene Adler maybe," rejoined Matt.

Cheeky sod, sitting in my kitchen, stealing my work product and belittling my efforts during a nightmare escape from injustice. For him it was just business as usual. For me, my world and life were turned upside down. "Apologize or you're off the next case!" I didn't give him a chance to respond however, as I noticed the time, "We gotta go. Food's done."

Matt lifted a platter to haul out to the car I rented for the job. "I see food. It's going to the rock n roll event. So where's the sex?" he asked with a mischievous grin.

My heart beat a little faster as I guessed, "This is going to be your first after-party, isn't it?"

About the Author

Stacey is the author of screenplays, TV shows, cookbooks, novels, academic books on the music industry, stage plays and children's stories. She lives in England and is a member of The Society of Authors, National Union of Journalists, New York State Bar and a Wednesday Night Quiz team at The Green Dragon. With Emma Hofberg she podcasts as Two Gone Blondes. www.shhh.media

Other Books by Stacey Haber:
The Rainbow Kitchen
Red Recipes From The Rainbow Kitchen
Orange Recipes From The Rainbow Kitchen
Yellow Recipes From The Rainbow Kitchen
A Painter Paints

Coming soon:
Lola's Cookbook – Sex, Food & Rock n Roll
A Gefilte Fish Out of Water
Green Recipes From The Rainbow Kitchen

BV - #0027 - 180225 - C0 - 210/148/10 - PB - 9781916036383 - Gloss Lamination